TO Moira
with best wishes
from
Robin Lloyd-Jones

20·2·94

FALLEN ANGELS

FALLEN ANGELS
Stories of Los Gamines

Robin Lloyd-Jones

CANONGATE PRESS

First published in Great Britain in 1992
by Canongate Press Plc,
14 Frederick Street, Edinburgh EH2 2HB.

The publishers acknowledge subsidy of the
Scottish Arts Council towards the
publication of this volume.

British Library Cataloguing-in-Publication Data
A catalogue record for this book is available from the
British Library.

ISBN 0 86241 320 6

Phototypeset by Hewer Text Composition Services,
Edinburgh.
Printed and bound in Great Britain by Billings, Worcester

Foreword

Angel, Angelina, Nelsón and the other people in this book are fictitious characters and the city in which they live is a fictitious city. However, everything that happens to Angel and his companions has happened, is happening and will continue to happen, in one form or another, to real street children. These tragedies are well documented in a number of reports by UNICEF and by the Anti-Slavery Society. Many of the things described I saw for myself in Bogota where I spent time getting to know the street kids. In my stories, however, I have not named the city in which they live because I do not wish to convey the impression that this problem is confined to one particular city or country. Street children are a worldwide phenomenon. Nobody knows for sure how many such children there are. UNICEF estimates that there are at least 30,000,000 children whose lives are similar to Angel's, and some sources put the figure as high as 80,000,000. One thing is certain: the number increases daily.

Many people in South America helped to make this book possible. In particular, I would like to thank the brothers Nelsón and Louis, aged ten and eight, for allowing me a glimpse of life on the streets—they have since disappeared and their whereabouts is no longer known; the real Angel (who taught himself to read and escaped from the streets to become a social

worker), in whose company I safely walked the forbidden quarters in the forbidden hours; Rosario Saavedra of
CINEP for many invaluable contacts; Javier de Nicolo
of the Bosconia-La Florida recovery programme; Father
Francisco de Roux (now in exile) for opening my eyes
to the misery of the barrios; and Marta Forero of the
University of the Andes for much excellent research,
advice and practical help. Finally, to the Scottish Arts
Council, who gave me a travel and research grant, I
record my gratitude.

                                        R.L-J.
                               February 1992

Contents

The Blood of the Saviour

The glowing orange halo slipped behind the pinnacle on which stood the Saviour of the World, an immense concrete figure, arms outstretched, blessing the city below it. Claudia sat on the crumbling sidewalk trying to sell the last of her bananas. Sometimes business picked up a little after sundown. Not until then had the poor of the city accumulated enough to buy their evening meal. Claudia thought about her two children, Angel and Angelina, waiting in their one-room shack in the barrio. Her evening sales would be the difference between whether she could give them rice and beans or only coffee thickened with flour.

Times had not always been so hard. She could remember the days when she had been able to purchase a basketful of bananas straight from the lorries that came in from the countryside and sell them door to door in the wealthier suburbs of the city—the kind of places where the cats had tails—where people were so rich that they'd buy a whole bunch. But it only takes a couple of bad days, a brief illness, a pressing debt and you haven't got the money to buy your stock for the day. So Claudia had been reduced to buying smaller quantities of bruised bananas, hawking them in a poorer part of the city. Now she had slid even further down the scale, selling small pieces, already peeled, cut from mouldy and blackened fruit, the unsold stock of those higher up the ladder. She sat in the backstreet gutters amongst other vendors whose prices rarely exceeded half a peso,

who sold cigarettes singly, matches split in two and tied
in half-dozen bundles, broken biscuits by the half-cup
and used coffee-grounds in twists of newspaper. Last
night her man, César, had taken yesterday's small profit
from her purse and spent it getting drunk. Without
sufficient capital to buy today's stock, she had lifted
her plaster statue of The Holy Lamb of God off the
shelf above the bed and taken it to the pawn shop on
the corner of Calle Octavia and Carrera Tercera.

By half-past ten she knew it was hopeless. Nobody
was buying her blackened, almost liquid offerings, now
encrusted with the day's grime. Rather than take home
what was left she would throw it away—that was how
hopeless it was. How was she going to buy food for her
children, regain posession of her precious statue and still
have enough for tomorrow's stock? She would sell her
blood. She'd done it before. She knew all about those
clinics where a healthy profit was made from the trade
in blood by asking few questions of those who sold it
to them and seldom adhering to regulations about the
maximum amount you were supposed to give at one
time. She walked the block and a half to the clinic,
knowing it would be open at this hour. This was a
peak time for them. On the wall of a building someone
had sprayed, in red letters a meter tall, 'FLN', the initials
of the outlawed guerrilla group, and below that were
the words 'Revolution Now!'. They had made several
attempts at assassinating El Presidente. The reprisals had
been savage. Claudia walked on. She knew, even with
her eyes shut, that she was in the poorer streets. The
unrepaired state of the road, the absence of traffic, the
way feet shuffled rather than stepped out smartly, the
sounds of children playing in the middle of the road
even at this hour. And you could always tell the kind
of district it was from the smell of the cooking. It
had been a long day and she was anxious about her

children alone in the shack. She pushed on past rows
of stalls selling barbecued meats, their charcoal grills
and kerosene lamps glowing in the dark. A taxi driver
lounged in the passenger seat of his car, door open, while
a little boy of about five shined his shoes and a syphilitic
girl of no more than thirteen tried to catch his eye.
Claudia thought about what food she would buy with
the money she'd get for her blood. Purchasing things in
small quantities was the expensive way of doing it, but
she never had more than a few coppers in hand at any one
time. The trouble was the poor couldn't afford the price
of poverty. A large poster outside a cinema announced,
'All this week: Los Vampiros'. A white-faced, fanged
monster stood jaws red and dripping, over a whole
family who were shrivelled and sucked dry.

Crossing the road to the clinic, she saw that a
street puppeteer had set up his quickly-collapsible stage
directly outside its entrance. The face of a glove puppet
slowly rose above the lower curtain; it had an apple-
cheeked, rustic face with a simple, honest expression.

'I, Ernesto, am not in this play I'm glad to say. It's
a load of rubbish. I advise you all to clear off. Go on!
It's not worth watching, I tell you.' He glanced around
furtively. Then, putting one hand to his mouth, whispered, 'What would you expect when that fool Busca
has had a hand in it? What, are you all still here? So
you're gluttons for punishment are you? Must be if you
put up with him.' He pointed to a grotesque caricature
of El Presidente which hung from the backcloth of the
stage, imitating the obligatory photograph religiously
displayed by every organisation or business.

Ernesto raised his finger. 'Sh! Here comes the blood-
thirsty doctor.'

Dr Acula entered left, dressed in clinical white. A
second figure, also dressed in white, entered from the
opposite side. This man, however, wore long flowing

robes. Dr Acula glared at him. 'Hey! Campesino! Bumpkin! You with the crown of thorns on your head! Gentlemen remove their headgear when they enter a high-class establishment!'

'In that case I'll keep it on.'

Enraged, Dr Acula hopped about the stage, managing, in the process, to back onto a hypodermic needle of horrific length, which made him hop about even more.

'Jesus Christ! Ah! Ow!'

'Yes? You called me?'

'Fool! You've come to offer your blood, I suppose?'

'I have. That was what I was sent to do.'

'You look a pretty anaemic specimen to me, but since you're here we'd better fill in the correct form . . . Name?'

'Jesus Christ.'

'Occupation?'

'Um . . . better put down "Carpenter".'

Dr Acula peered closely at the nail marks in the palms of Jesus's hands.

'Dios! I've heard of clumsy carpenters hitting their thumb with a hammer, but— '

'How much are you paying for blood these days?'

'Depends what blood type you are. Group A is one thousand pesos per litre. B negative is— '

'I'm not sure what group mine is. It's the kind that washes away sins . . . you know . . . the kind that gives salvation to those who truly repent and . . .'

'Sorry! No demand for that type.' Dr Acula nodded towards El Presidente. 'No demand at all. Not among my clients, anyway.'

They haggled and eventually settled on a whole bodyful for thirty pieces of silver.

Claudia entered the clinic. When she emerged, a little

after midnight, she felt weak, leaden-legged and dizzy. It was early Sunday morning; a nearby church was crowded with the poor of the neighbourhood, mainly women, attending midnight Mass, people who rose early and worked all day, even on Sundays and had no other time to go. The door of the church was open, light flooding out of it. Over the heads of the ragged beggars who sat on the steps Claudia could see the faithful receiving Holy Communion.

'This is my blood. Drink this in remembrance of me,' the priest intoned. 'This is my blood . . .'

Claudia felt in her bag until her fingers encountered her pawn ticket. Now she could redeem her Holy Lamb of God and restore him to his shelf where he would watch over her children as they slept.

Happy Days

Angel glanced up, hope and fear colliding in his heart with a thump. Whose footsteps were approaching the shack? The clock in the Plaza de Bolívar struck midnight. Angel was beginning to panic. They were behind schedule with the dolls. That was what happened when you got to be ten years old—you got put in charge of things, made responsible, punished when they went wrong. He touched the side of his swollen face. If they were short of the target, César would fly into one of his rages and thrash Angel with the buckle end of his heavy belt. To add to his troubles, Angelina had diarrhoea again. Any minute now she'd start pretending she was Gatita the kitten. Were eight-year-old girls always so difficult or was it just his sister?

One hundred and fifty dolls a week was the quota, the hair to be threaded through the perforations in the head, glued from the inside and the head screwed onto the body. 'Crying dolls with real hair' was how they were advertised by Happydays Inc. Happydays paid two pesos per doll—which was more like one peso per doll after you had bought from them the special glue, the brushes, the solvent and the threading hook, and you had paid for any dolls that were damaged or not returned. The weekly profit margin was seldom more than one hundred and twenty pesos, hardly more than the price of a couple of glasses of fiery aguardiente, which was exactly what it was spent on when César got his hands on it. Mewing, Angelina curled her hands into paws. 'Gatita is tired. Gatita wants to stop now.'

'Well, she can't!'

In her own voice Angelina whined, 'But Gatita says her head hurts and her tummy hurts and . . .'

'Fuck Gatita! If that girl of three down the lane can sort sweetie papers all day, surely you can . . . Oh, what's the use? Tell Gatita she can take a rest.'

One of these days, when there was time, instead of making stupid dolls, he'd make a kite for himself. There weren't many things he could call his very own: the clothes he wore, the figure of Santa Teresa, his collection of bottle-tops and the occasional home-made toy which he always ended up exchanging for food.

More footsteps . . . too steady to be César's, not weary enough to be his mother's. She was always out till this hour, trying to sell the last of the bananas. She was always tired. Angel couldn't think when he had last heard her laugh. The one bare bulb which lit the room began flickering, making it difficult to see what they were doing. If it expired, he'd fall behind on the quota even more and they didn't have a spare bulb, nor was there much chance of borrowing one. Probably the flickering was because of the state of the line running from their shack, looping from branch to branch, and from one tottering pole to the next until it linked with the main electric cable. Or perhaps something was frying on the connecting point, an electrocuted bird—or worse. About once a week someone in their barrio was killed or maimed trying illegally to fix a line to the main cable.

Angel's eyes could stay away from it no longer—the sheet of newspaper covering the crack above the door. There was an advertisement on it, a picture of a steaming bowl of rice, rich with peas, egg, chunks of chicken and chopped ham. Despite the fumes from the glue and the solvent, Angel could smell that plate of food as if it was on the table in front of him. His stomach contracted painfully.

All the walls were covered with newspaper, it absorbed the damp and had a permanently soggy look. When the mud plaster cracked the newspaper split and peeled at the edges. Of much tougher material were the posters which could be stripped from the hoardings before the paste was dry—like the one above the sink which covered a large crumbling patch on the wall. It was made of the same kind of paper as those glossy magazines about films and the luxurious lives of their stars. Mercedes, their neighbour, worked as a maid for an employer who let her take the old ones home. Mercedes and Angel's mother would look through them together, exclaiming over the beautiful rooms, the furniture, the clothes worn by the women. If there was a leak in the roof one of these magazines, pushed tight against a rafter, was much better than a piece of cardboard, which soon became soggy, and dripped and sagged.

The hairs on the end of Angel's hook became entangled. He was trying to work too fast, he knew it. The glue was making his eyes run and he was too hungry to go on working. Every part of him felt empty, so empty and hollow that he echoed and buzzed with surges of dizziness. It was hopeless trying to continue with the dolls. Angelina was falling asleep over her work and she had messed her underwear again, although she would pretend she hadn't. Her head jerked up and she gave one of her nervous, anxious-to-please smiles.

'Don't be cross. I wasn't asleep, not really, was I, Gatita?'

'We might as well stop,' Angel said.

They were more than a day behind on their schedule. Tomorrow he'd have to sub-contract some of the work. Taking a smaller profit was better than losing the work altogether for not fulfilling the quota agreed with Happydays. He knew a girl in the 'Swamp', the cardboard and sacking section of the barrio, who would gladly do a day's work for the price of a bowl of soup.

'Angel, what do you think mama will bring us to eat?'

'How should I know?'

'Do you think . . . you know . . . he . . . will be back early today or not?'

Angel didn't reply. The time between César reaching the shack and his mother's return, the time when César was alone with them, was the unpredictable, dangerous time. Sometimes it was as much as two hours, sometimes it was only a few minutes, depending on how soon César's drinking money ran out. As he did every night, Angel weighed up the possibilities. If César was late, the time alone with him would be shorter, but he would have drunk more and be more violent.

Angelina began to cry. 'Gatita is hungry!'

'Damn you, Angelina, shut up!'

The panic in Angel's voice made Angelina cry all the more.

'Please don't,' Angel implored. César didn't like too much noise when he came in and he would punish Angel for not keeping his sister quiet. 'I love you! I love you!' Angel pleaded, raining anxious kisses on her face. 'Listen, you can have some of my food tonight if you stop.'

Angelina sniffed hard, wiping her nose with a black, glue-encrusted finger. 'How much is some?'

'Plenty, I promise.'

Angelina stopped crying. Angel took the broom from behind the door and poked it under the bed, ramming it back and forth with a vigorous pumping action to scare off the rats. They nested in the space between the outer planks of the shack and the mud and lath inner wall. For a large part of the day, though, they squatted under the bed scratching at the underside of the wire frame, or gnawing at the rusty metal box in which Santa Teresa lay. They gnawed at the box because inside it there was also a candle. Angel hooked out the box with the broom. He put the box on the table, propped up Santa Teresa and set up the candle. Maybe, if he took a little nibble at the candle himself, it would stop the hunger which gnawed at him. All that rich grease and fat with a texture like hard cheese. He imagined his teeth biting into it, then remembered he'd tried it before and been sick. Angelina, who had finished packing away the dolls and the hair, stood beside him.

'Can I light the candle?'

'No.'

'Can I blow out the match, then?'

'OK.'

Angel lit the candle and handed the burning match to Angelina. He crossed himself and prayed to Santa Teresa, but Santa Teresa didn't always listen to his entreaties. Was it because he gave her only one minute of the lit candle, while, for the bugs, the candle burned much longer, making them crack and explode like dry twigs? The bugs lived in the woodwork. They gave off a strong, sharp smell. You could always sniff out a house that had bugs. It was essential to kill them off before they found their way into the mattress. The legs of the bed stood in bowls of kerosine, but the bugs crawled along the ceiling and then dropped on to the bed. Angel was responsible for burning them out of the woodwork with the candle, then sealing the holes with the hot wax. That was why his mother bought a candle once a week. She didn't know about the stolen minute for Santa Teresa. Another fine calculation, another delicate counter-balance of the certainty of bug-bites and the off-chance that Santa Teresa might be disposed to notice him.

'Another thirty seconds for you, Santa Teresa. Hear me this time. Please hear me.'

Santa Teresa was a damaged Happydays doll. Her halo, the jagged top of an opened can, shone in the candle light. Tears ran down Santa Teresa's face. When the tear reservoirs inside the head were filled, the dolls cried on being tilted.

Angelina lurched sleepily against the table, knocking the candle over. It rolled off the edge of the table and fell into a bottom drawer which was open just wide enough to receive it. She wrenched at the drawer, but it was jammed. Smoke writhed upwards.

'Help me, Angel!'

Together they tugged at the drawer. Smoke was pouring out, flames beginning to flicker.

'Water, Angelina! Get some water! Hurry for Christ's sake!'

Angelina returned with a bowl slopping at the edge. Angel seized it from her and emptied the water through the crack. The flames went out, the smoke subsided.

'Dios mío!' Angel moaned.

César's best clothes had been in the drawer. Angelina said nothing, her arms rising and falling at her sides like the wings of a wounded bird. The heavy padlock rattled and thumped against the door. A wet patch spread across the crotch of Angel's threadbare jeans, urine running in rivulets over the uneven mud floor and seeping under the chipped sink. There was only one way he knew to make the terror stop. Reaching for the Happydays solvent, he tucked it down the front of his torn and soiled jersey, then, stretching the garment over his head into a kind of canopy, he retired into a world of his own, inhaling deeply until everything dissolved into beautiful patterns, into dreams in which Santa Teresa answered all his prayers.

Open Veins

Moonlit figures swayed in single file across the mountainside. A cough, a curse, a rasping breath and odours like gasses from an overtaxed digestive system belched from the mouths of dark tunnels in El Monton de Plata. Nelsón followed his father and the other miners up the stony path. Midnight to seven in the morning was the normal shift for a boy of twelve. His worn and faded overalls, handed down from his father, were several sizes too big, rolled up at sleeve and trouser and with the seat of the pants nearly dragging on the ground. But Nelsón swaggered inside them because they were proper miners' overalls. If only he had boots instead of old canvas sneakers, the kind with steel toe-caps. Then he'd be the star of the lane's football games, crunching bare feet under his hobnails and biffing the tin can out of sight. It wouldn't happen, of course. In his barrio, nobody had that kind of money. But to dream costs nothing, *soñar no cuesta nada*.

The path they followed zig-zagged up the steep slope towards their particular dark hole in the hillside. From vents in the rock reddish-brown cuprous liquid seeped out like blood from a wound. They walked slowly because Jorge, Nelsón's father, didn't breathe too well. Sometimes, when their hours of rest coincided, Nelsón would lie awake in the family bed listening to his father fighting for breath, listening to the sounds of a man slowly suffocating.

A miner descending the track greeted Jorge. 'Buenas
tardes! Qué tal?'

Jorge grunted a reply, his chest heaving.

The man said, 'When the shift ends, are you going to
the meeting?'

'No, not I. Celso is representing us.'

'I thought it would have been you, Jorge. You would
have been the one to speak for the cause, to win people
round.'

Jorge avoided the man's eyes and mumbled, 'You
know how it is . . . I have a family and . . .'

Nelsón walked ahead. All this talk about the miners
joining together to form a union made him uneasy.
There was always tension in the air whenever the topic
came up.

The path angled upwards across a man-made scree of
slag and spoil. Nelsón had worked in the mine several
months before discovering it wasn't silver they were
mining but copper, tin and zinc. The silver had long
since been worked out, leaving a hillside honeycombed
with empty shafts and tunnels. Only the name now
carried hints of former glory—*El Monton de Plata*,
the Silver Mountain. With the rising value of copper, tin and zinc on the world market, the mines
had reopened to extract what the conquistadores had
spurned. Open veins. That was what his father called
those miles of underground passages and abandoned
shafts. Open veins.

'The life-blood of our country drained from us to give
new life to another continent.'

People listened when his father spoke. He was a
driller and people paid heed to drillers. They were the
elite of the underground workers. People listened and
heard the bubbling in his lungs, a mark of his years
in the mines which lent weight to his failing voice.
Sometimes, when Nelsón wanted to appear grown up,

he would imitate the voice and the round-shouldered, hollow-chested stance.

The path brought them to a quarried shelf upon which there squatted a square windowless building of corrugated iron, topped by a wooden cross. Nelsón and Jorge entered the little chapel and knelt on the rough stone floor at the end of a line of men and boys. More than sixty different companies mined El Monton de Plata. Some of the kneeling men were *campesinos*, peasants who leased the mining rights on a percentage basis and used their own children to work underground. Others were employed in the bigger mines such as *El Cinquenta*, Shaft Fifty, where Nelsón and his father worked. Nearly all the boys who worked in the mines did the night shift because the one-teacher schools in the poor barrios surrounding the city functioned from eight in the morning till midday and it was an offence for employers to prevent children from attending elementary school. To employ children under fifteen in heavy industries like mining was also an offence. It said so in the statute books.

'But you have to understand, Nelsón, that enforcing laws like that might damage the economic health of the country,' Jorge would say. And then he would give one of his bitter laughs which sounded like a car trying to start on a run-down battery.

They shuffled forward on their knees towards a stone altar on which candles flickered. Arriving at the front of the line, Jorge drew from his haversack two flat maize cakes which his wife had made. He crossed himself and placed one cake in front of the statue of the Virgin of the Mineshaft and the other in front of *El Señor de los Compadres*, the favourite saint of the miners. The cakes reminded Nelsón how hungry he was, but he knew the importance of an offering like that. The protection racket was the same the world over.

The miners stood in groups, masking their fear by
casually spitting, shouting mock insults to each other,
rough-housing and laughing loudly—anything to keep
at bay the dark, gaping mouth ready to swallow you, the
knots tightening in the stomach, the fear of falling rock,
the panic that you might never smell fresh air again. The
mayordomo shouted out the instructions. Jorge to drill
at level 320 with old Carlos; Nelsón, Raul and Garcia
to load and push the trolleys on level 321 where Celso
was drilling; Ramon, a boy of seven, to work the seam
on 321 East with a handpick. He was the only one
small enough to squeeze into the eighteen-inch high
tunnel; Simon, the carpenter, to box in the connecting
shaft between levels 318 and 319 which had partially
collapsed . . .

The evening shift was coming up, tired, silent men
who vanished into the night. A gang was working the
capstan, round and round, muscles straining, slowly
winching up the rusty iron trucks one by one. There
was a diesel-driven winch, but last week it had seized
up and stalled causing a truck to go crashing backwards
down the steep tunnel. A boy had been killed.

Nelsón huddled in the rattling, bumping, swaying
truck with four other boys, keeping his head below the
rim to avoid being decapitated by the tunnel roof. The
circle of starlit sky shrank to the size of a five-peso piece,
then disappeared. Nelsón tensed as they swept round a
bend. Surely, this time, they would be de-railed. At level
320, the truck slowed and bumped to a halt. Nelsón
clambered out, carrying the shovel and bicycle lamp
handed out by the mayordomo.

This was where the image of Tío stood, carved out
of a rock carried up from the deepest part of the mine.
Above ground the saints were prayed to for safety, but
down here the earth gods held sway. Tío was squat,
half human, half animal, with horns like a bull and an

enormous phallus. Fear makes men impotent, a state which could only be remedied by appealing to Tío. Nelsón joined his father who had made the descent several trucks earlier. Jorge produced a metal hip-flask and poured aguardiente, the fiery local brandy, over Tío's head.

'May I work without losing the vein, may my drill tear at the rock like your horns.'

Nelsón placed a cigarillo in Tío's mouth and silently asked Tío to give him the strength to fill more than his quota of trucks and earn a bonus. It wasn't easy to do. You started off well, but then you got slower and slower. His father had regularly earned a bonus at the same job when he was a youngster, so the other men kept reminding him.

The mayordomo stood in front of Jorge, a sneer on his face. He was a burly man and the only one wearing a helmet. He wore it as a mark of authority rather than out of any concern for safety.

'Last time you were on, so I'm told, you broke a drilling piece!'

'It was old and worn, Señor el mayordomo.'

'You're the one that's old and worn, maybe too old for the job. Listen, maleta caquero, it's coming out of your wages and if it happens again I'm taking you off the drilling, understand?'

'Yes, señor.'

El mayordomo swaggered off. Jorge stood there, hands hanging by his side, fists clenching and un-clenching. Nelsón slunk away. His father didn't hit him often, but being witness to his humiliation made this a dangerous time. Better to pretend he hadn't seen it. He hated the mayordomo and right now, in a different way, he hated his father too. Why hadn't papa stood up for himself? His own father, so tough, so brave.

Nelsón sought out Garcia and Raul, and together they began the descent of the vertical ventilation shaft connecting levels 320 and 321. The shaft was four-sided, boxed by rotting timbers. Being narrow enough to climb down with the back braced against one wall and the feet against the other, no ladder was provided. They worked their way down in the dark so as to preserve their lamp batteries, otherwise they never lasted the full shift. The safest plan in a vertical shaft was to keep close together. That way, if the top person dislodged any loose rock from the places where the timbers had burst apart, it didn't gather much momentum before hitting those below.

Nelsón dug his nails into the soft, waterlogged timber and tried to get a grip with his feet on the slimy log on the opposite wall. Despite the draught of air which was being sucked down the shaft, he was sweating, the sweat of anxiety rather than exertion. Whichever position you were in, first, last, or middle, the others always seemed to be going too fast, either leaving you behind or treading on you from above. Of course, you pretended the pace was just fine.

Arriving at the bottom, Nelsón dropped through the square hole into the passage at level 321. He knew, without turning on his lamp, that the overhead beams were sagging, that white, mouldy growths sprouted from them and that looping from one splintered upright prop to the next were the air hoses. One carried the compressed air for the drills, while the other, made of ordinary clear polythene sheet, was supposed to carry fresh air to those parts of the mine furthest from the ventilation shafts. There were so many holes and tears in it, however, that most of the air was dissipated long before it reached the places it was most needed. A muffled explosion rumbled somewhere deep below them. The rock shivered, the timbers groaned. They walked in single file, keeping to the middle, where the roof was just high enough.

'It's somewhere along here,' Garcia said.

Even after working years in the mine people got lost. The tunnels and passages were never the same from one month to the next, new ones being excavated and others closing down because of rock falls, flooding or gasses. At a fork where the rails divided, they hesitated. Then the shattering din of the drill started up to guide them to the workface.

As they approached, Celso, the driller, gave them a quick sideways glance. Goggles protected his eyes and a scarf covered his ears to deaden the noise. He nodded at them: words could not compete with the clamour of the machine, the whine and scream of the drilling piece biting into the rock, the air hissing through the hose. The heavy pneumatic drill was supported by a metal stand, but even then it kicked and bucked and vibrated, making Celso's face quiver as if he was blubbering or having a fit.

The three boys worked behind Celso, shovelling the loosened ore into the trucks. Water and clay oozed from the rock, soaking their feet. Nelsón slid his shovel into the muddy heap. It was always heavier when it was wet. Push the shovel forward, use the knee behind the elbow, lift and swing. Push, lift and swing. Try to maintain a rhythm. It was a race, a race to keep up with the drill, a race to hold your own with Garcia and Raul, a race against the clock with six trucks to be filled and pushed to the surface before the end of the shift.

A flying fragment of rock sliced into Celso's arm. He worked on, oblivious to the injury, his whole body numbed by the juddering and jarring. 'You're falling behind!' Garcia shouted in Nelsón's ear. Nelsón stepped up the rhythm. How long till the break? Count off the shovel-loads in fives. One sodding shovel-load,

two sodding shovel-loads, three . . . the drilling piece
snapped in two. The drill crashed off its stand onto
Celso, the jagged stump of the drilling piece ploughing
across his chest, shoulder and neck. An absence of
noise. The drill silent. Then Celso hoarsely calling,
'No! Please, no! No . . .' Folds of severed flesh hung
from him, exposing white bone. Blood was spraying
from his neck into the mud and clay, one hue of red
mingling with another.

The three boys stared at Celso. Garcia broke the spell.
'You go, Raul. Run for help. Go on, go!'

With difficulty, Garcia and Nelsón raised Celso to his
feet and helped him slump into an empty truck, while
he dripped blood over them and swore and snarled at
them for their clumsiness.

'Right! Get pushing!' Garcia commanded, setting his
own shoulder to the back of the truck. 'And what the hell
are you snivelling for? You're not the one who's hurt!'

Nelsón put his head down and pushed. He didn't
know why he was crying, he just was.

'We only . . . filled three . . . trucks,' Garcia panted.

'And that's all we'll fucking well be . . . paid for . . .
I'll bet!'

'Yeah, I'll bet!' Nelsón growled. It was a familiar,
comforting grievance, easier to handle.

'Ojo! Ojo!'

Garcia's breathless cry echoed down the passage,
warning people of their approach, giving them time
to press themselves into one of the alcoves, out of
the path of the truck. But there was nobody ahead,
nobody to offer to push, nobody to lift the responsibility
from them.

'Is he alright, Garcia? Why's he so quiet?'

'How should I fucking know? Keep pushing!'

Celso stirred and groaned.

'Ojo! Ojo!' Garcia shouted into the darkness.

'Why isn't there any help coming, Garcia? Where are the people Raul went to fetch?'

'Shut up and push!'

'Nelsón,' Celso mumbled. 'Nelsón . . . tell your father something for me.'

'Yes, señor?'

'About the meeting . . . tell him he'll have to take my place. He's the only one, nobody else . . . tell him I said so. It's important . . . tell him.'

Garcia shone his lamp on Celso's face.

'I think he's fainted.'

Then lights were flickering in the distance and men's voices were calling to them.

Nelsón shielded his eyes as the iron truck emerged into the early-morning light. The men were at the capstan again, winching up the trucks, plodding round and round. There were mounds of spoil heaped around the tunnel openings, turning the hillside into a crazy quilt of varying colours, pink, lilac, purple, ochre, gray, gold, brown. Already, a small army of women and children were picking bird-like through this rubble, gleaning a living from the mineral debris. Nelsón looked around for his father. Stooping, he picked up a rock and smashed it against a larger boulder. Why did that estupido Celso have to have an accident? Now his father would be going to the meeting instead of Celso. He

hated the meeting. Each time his father had mentioned it
at home there'd been a quarrel and his mother had cried.
And now it was going to prevent his father keeping him
company on the bus. Usually there was a left-over piece
of bread in his father's pocket and a warm shoulder to
fall asleep against.

'Papa!'

Jorge didn't look round, but kept his back turned to
Nelsón, his chest heaving, a handkerchief pressed to his
mouth. Nelsón plucked at his sleeve.

'Papa, Celso said to tell you that— '

Jorge jerked his arm free. 'Not now!' Nelsón slumped
onto a pile of pit-props but then his father's rough hand
reached out and patted Nelsón's shouder.

'So what's on your mind, son?'

Nelsón told him about the accident and about what
Celso had said. Jorge nodded.

'Yes, I heard about it. I . . . I was half expecting some
sort of message like that. Some things in life pursue you.'
He gave one of his bitter, wheezing laughs. 'You can't
seem to evade them. I'll walk with you as far as the
chapel. That's where the meeting's to be, I think.' Then,
with a friendly punch, 'You'd better get going or you'll
be late for school. We wouldn't want that, would we?'

Nelsón started down the slope towards the place
where the buses left.

'And Nelsón,' he called. Nelsón turned.

'Yes, Papa?'

'Nothing, son. Adiós.'

As Nelsón waited for the bus the sun was just clearing
the tops of the Palace of Justice, the Hilton skyscraper
and the high modern offices of the multinational companies. He saw a helicopter fly overhead, saw it land near
the little chapel on the hillside and disgorge soldiers, then
he heard prolonged bursts of automatic fire—a sound
which would echo repeatedly in his mind.

The Miracle Play

'Grunni! Grunnaaa! My name is Caciquismo!' The dragon, a glove puppet, wearing a waistcoat of stars and stripes, hopped and swivelled around the make-shift theatre, continually returning to a pile of gold. Overhead, a balloon made from twin circles of tin-foil twisted in the breeze, presenting alternately a sad face and a funny face. A crowd had gathered on the sidewalk, attracted by the balloon which Busca always hoisted to signal when one of his puppet shows was about to begin.

The dragon growled in a deep voice, 'El Dragón Caciquismo brings to you a miracle play!' The dragon gave a swish of its tail and beat a drum. Boom! Boom! Up popped a small, red-faced man, in a woolly cap and long nightgown.

'Hurrah! Hurrah! I love miracles, don't you?' He bowed to the audience. 'My name is Ernesto. And with the price of food the way it is, we could do with a miracle or two, couldn't we?'

With a flick of its tail the dragon knocked Ernesto flat.

'Silence, little man! I do all the talking here!'

Caciquismo pawed his pile of gold lovingly and rolled and wriggled on it, scratching his back and belly. 'Grunni, grunnaaa!'

Ernesto sat up and clapped his hand to his forehead. 'Dios mío! I've forgotten something important!' He pointed straight at the audience. 'Can you whistle through your fingers?'

'Sí . . . Sí señor, sí señor Ernesto.'

'Well, let's hear you then, let's hear you! Louder! That's better!' Ernesto jumped about the stage. 'Bravo! Bravo!' Then tripped over the dragon's tail, falling flat again. 'What do you say, you good people out there, will you be our lookout?' He leant forward and said in a loud whisper, 'You see, la policia don't like us.' Boom! Boom! went the drum at a twitch of Caciquismo's tail. 'Which reminds me,' Ernesto said. 'What has the worst sting? Come on reptile, tell me that!'

Caciquismo rolled his head. 'A bee?'

'No.'

'A snake?'

'No. The answer is la policia.'

'La policia?'

'Yes. When one of them stung my daughter she swelled right up in front. Yes, there's no doubt about it—our police are the best money can buy.' Boom! Boom! 'Dios mio, now I've forgotten my lines! Does anyone know my lines?' cried a distraught Ernesto. The dragon held up a prompt card behind Ernesto's back.

A woman in the crowd read out, 'Tell us Señor Caciquismo, why is this a miracle play?'

'Grunni! Grunnaa! Because it's about the wonderful economic miracle our country is experiencing.'

While Ernesto continued to look for his lines, searching his clothing, looking up the dragon's backside, poking his head into it's mouth, another prompt card came up. The crowd chorused on Ernesto's behalf: 'What economic miracle? There has been no economic miracle!'

'Grunni! Grunnaa! What's that I hear? Is it the rumbling of empty bellies, or did someone speak? Listen you ignorant, ill-fed rabble, don't argue with me, I'm telling you—there's been an economic miracle. And that's official.'

Boom! Boom!

'Oh no there hasn't!' Ernesto protested.

'Oh yes there has!' growled the dragon.

Encouraged by Ernesto, the crowd joined him. 'Oh no there hasn't!'

Ernesto hung right out of the stage and, with a quick movement, seemed to pluck a piece of paper from the mouth of a grubby boy.

'Ah! Here are my words. It says here, "I'm lost for words"!' He popped below the stage to reappear with a balloon held to his mouth which was slowly and inexorably expanding. 'So let me tell you about inflation since you don't seem to recognise it when it . . . hits you on the nose!'

'Ouch! Grunni! Grunnaa!'

'Yes, the price of everything's going up. Why, only last month a kidnapped German Ambassador was worth ten political prisoners. This month, who knows—twenty, thirty, forty— ' Bang went the balloon. 'So, tell us you overgrown worm, tell us of this miracle. Give us just one example.'

'Well,' said the dragon, shifting uneasily on its pile of gold. 'Well, we're a fast-developing country.'

'Yes, we're fast developing poverty and misery.'

'And,' Boom! Boom! 'exports are booming.'

'Yes, I must agree, Señor Caciquismo. By working for slave wages for foreign companies we export our health, our happiness, our lives.'

Caciquismo bit off Ernesto's head and swallowed it.

'Ah! Suddenly I see it.' exclaimed the head from inside the dragon.

'See what?' asked the headless Ernesto, tripping over the dragon's tail once more. 'I see nothing.'

'There has indeed been a miracle,' said the disembodied head to the headless body.

'Praise the Lord!'

'The miracle is the survival of poverty. It is the wonder of the modern world. Amongst all this wealth, this new technology, this record productivity, it bears a charmed life.'

The dragon gave a loud belch and out rolled Ernesto's head, still wearing its woolly cap. Ernesto picked up his head and, leaning out again, dropped it into the lap of the grubby boy.

'This lad,' Ernesto shouted, 'will now pass among you with my head. Give generously for the cause.' *What* cause he didn't say.

'Grunni! Grunnaa!' growled Caciquismo, interrupting the counting of his gold. 'That stingy lot give anything? Huh! That certainly would be a miracle.'

Just Pretend

Chinche was nine, smaller than most boys of his age, a forest Indian. When their part of the forest was burned, Chinche's parents had sold him, then five years old, to a man who grew carnations in a valley on the other side of the mountains, about thirty miles from the city. Chinche had been forced to work twelve hours a day for the past four years, in the heat and humidity of the plastic greenhouses. With no protective mask or safety precautions of any kind, Chinche and the other children were made to spray the young buds with toxic pesticides. It was important that the buds came to full bloom in perfect condition. Inside this suffocating, plastic bubble, grew carnations of a pink and red variety, much the same colours as the blood and bits of lung which Chinche's friend had started coughing up. It had frightened Chinche so much that he ran away. In the last five days he had walked across the mountains and through the countryside, with hardly a bite to eat, until he had reached the city.

Chinche stood on the kerb, bewildered and excited by the traffic, the noise, the bustle. Close by was a stall selling arepas. Their savoury smell conjured up tantalising visions of rich dark meat inside pastry which was soft and warm in the mouth and was filling, so filling. He was wondering whether to snatch and run when a BMW pulled up at the kerb. The window slid open of its own accord. An arm lolled from the

window—heavy gold rings, gold watch and bracelet,
gold cuff-links—and lazily beckoned Chinche.

'What's your name, kid?'

'Chinche, señor.'

'Well, Chinche, how would you like one of those
arepas?' He called the vendor over. 'A big one for my
young friend here.'

Chinche snatched it from the vendor, tearing at it with
his teeth.

'Gracias señor,' he mumbled through a stuffed mouth.
'That's a beautiful car you have.'

'Like a ride in it? A couple of blocks maybe? Climb
in, you can finish your arepa as we go along.'

Chinche had never been in a car before and he was
in the front seat too! The upholstery was deep and soft
and made of a leather which gave out the same kind
of smell that wafted on to the street from the luxury
stores on Avenida Americano. The BMW eased into
the mainstream of the traffic.

'Where are we going?' Chinche asked.

The man winked and smiled.

'I'm always on the lookout for talent . . . and you've
got something, Chinche. Ever been in a film?'

'A film! Wow! Am I going to be in a film?'

'Maybe . . . We'll see. There'll be a few screen tests
first. Some kids get scared in front of the camera. Not
you, though. I can see you're not frightened to try
anything new. I could tell that as soon as I spotted
you. Call me Rico, by the way, we film folk are one
big family.'

'What kind of film?'

Rico weaved skilfully through the multitude of buses
which fought a private war with each other. Chinche
repeated the question. Rico handed him a gold cigarette
case, then a gold lighter.

'Here, help yourself and light one for me—and keep

the lighter, Chinche. A present from me. I help you and
you help me, like I say, one big family. We do anything
for each other, verdad?' As Rico accelerated past a
donkey cart laden with melons he flicked open a tray
of tapes. 'All the latest hits. Play anything you want.'

Chinche didn't want to admit he'd no idea how to
operate a cassette player.

'My fingers are greasy with the arepa.'

Rico hid a smile and pushed a cassette into the slot.

'I expect a smart kid like you gets around. Never at
a loss for a few crisp notes in your pocket, verdad?'

Chinche gave what he hoped was a knowing smile
and spread himself casually along the seat, tapping his
fingers on the soft leather in time to the music.

Rico said, 'I find, don't you, that the BMW accelerates
better than the Mercedes?' Chinche agreed, one man of
the world to another. 'Well, Chinche, before we do
anything else I expect you'd like something more to
eat, verdad? And a little wine? You do drink wine,
don't you?'

'Sure, Rico.' Chinche met Rico's eye with a new-
found confidence: a really wised-up guy like Rico liked
him, thought he was OK. That was more intoxicating
than any wine could ever be.

In Rico's apartment, Chinche sank into the fat cush-
ions on the sofa. The hot bath had been sheer luxury, so
different from washing in cold water in a cracked and
greasy sink shared with a dozen or more other children.
A bath followed by food and wine—he felt very happy.
And his new clothes were marvellously light and soft on
the skin. Rico had been so generous, helping him select
something from the wardrobe full of amazing clothes
like nothing he'd ever seen before, the kind of things,
Rico said, that up-and-coming young film stars wore.
Chinche had hesitated just a second over the short,
flimsy tunic. But Rico was right, of course—anyone

who didn't enjoy fun clothes like these would have to
be a very boring kind of person. Rico showed him the
camera mounted on a tripod, with its flash-gun and
reflector hood.

'You're going to be a natural in front of the camera, I
can see that. A real talent for it. That's rare, you know.'
Rico produced a different cigarette case, one in which
were four hand-rolled cigarettes.

'Are you old enough to smoke a little grass?'

'Of course I am,' Chinche exclaimed indignantly, taking one and manipulating his gold lighter into life. They
smoked with long, slow inhalations and even longer,
slower exhalations through lips that felt suddenly alive
and supersensitive. From a cassette player a trumpet solo
uncoiled in golden snakes, while the traffic snarled in the
streets and a vendor shouted monotonously, 'Avocados,
veinte pesos!', the sounds uniting into some mystic
harmony of their own and swelling into bubbles of
ever-changing colours which merged with each other
and melted the outlines of all hard-edged objects, gradually absorbing them. Rico laughed softly, a laugh which
came in bluish, brownish waves.

'There are some kids who come here expecting to be
turned into child stars and they haven't a hope. They're
simply wasting my time because they don't understand.
So it's a real pleasure to meet a kid like you who I
know isn't going to let me down, who understands
about these photographs . . . that they're only a bit of
fun, just pretending, fairy tales for adults, that's all. No
problem to someone like you who knows the score,
verdad?'

'Sure, no sweat,' said a voice, which Chinche thought
might have been his own.

'Yeah, that's all it is, Chinche . . . just a bit of fun,
just pretending. No harm in that, is there?'

The telephone rang. Rico cursed.

'I'd better answer it. That'll be New York.'

He crossed the room and picked up the receiver.
While he was talking, Chinche discovered a couple of
magazines down the back of a sofa. He turned the pages
. . . a nude girl of about eight or nine with her legs open,
staring knowingly at the camera; a naked baby sitting
on a lap from which rose an erect penis; a close-up of a
hairy adult anus into which a child's hand was pushing
a dildo.

'Don't worry,' Rico was saying into the phone,
'there's plenty of fresh talent at this end . . . yeah, the
usual route . . . yeah, a special edition . . . of course it
costs more for specialist tastes like that . . . OK, cash
on delivery . . .'

Chinche turned another page. The boy in the photo-graph was dressed in a tunic very like the one he was wearing. The boy was kneeling at an altar as if taking the sacrament at communion, eyes shut, mouth open to receive the Host, except that what was being thrust into his mouth was a big, fat penis.

Chinche's heart was pounding under his ribs. 'Just pretending,' Rico had said. Supposing it wasn't pre-tending? Besides, where did pretending end and really doing it begin? He'd change and leave. Perhaps he could slip away while Rico was on the phone.

His clothes were in the bedroom. He wandered casually through, then quickly began unbuttoning the tunic. It was halfway over his head when he sensed a presence bearing down on him. Rip! Head free, breathing hard. Rico was standing very close to him, his eyes reproachful, his voice very soft.

'You want to try a different costume, perhaps?'

'Well . . . I'm not sure that . . .'

'Not sure, eh? I like a boy who doesn't rush into things. Shows good sense. Nobody puts one over on you, I bet.'

Rico smiled admiringly at him and put a friendly arm on his shoulder. Chinche hoped Rico wouldn't feel him trembling, or sense the stupid alarm bells that suddenly shrilled in the back of his brain: he didn't want to give the impression that he was some kind of unsophisticated rústico.

'Come on, relax man! Take some more grass. That's it. It's top quality grass that, you know . . . yeah it certainly is. It's Panama Red.'

Chinche listened while Rico talked knowledgably about Santa Marta Gold, Blue Sky Blonde, Red Dot and Mango Viche, and about the differences between high altitude and low altitude strains of marijuana. It was the kind of thing a sharp city lad would be expected to know about, so he pursed his lips shrewdly and nodded wisely.

'I thought we'd try a few shots with you as you are, show off those good strong muscles of yours, eh?'

Chinche hugged his naked torso, suspicion scurrying out from dark holes.

'Rico, I don't know, I'm not . . .'

Rico sighed heavily. The telephone rang again. Rico hesitated then went through to the other room, but left the door open so that he could see Chinche. His conversation with someone called Pedro became more and more heated. Rico began walking up and down, looking only occasionally at Chinche. Now he had turned his back to reach for a file.

Quietly Chinche released the catch on the window and eased it open. Then, grabbing his clothes, he ducked through the opening onto a fire-escape and made for the street, the Panama Red still tingling in his brain.

Too late he realised he'd left the gold cigarette lighter behind. It probably wasn't solid gold anyway, gold-plated more like. Never mind, only his first day in the city and already he'd had a ride in a flash car! He skipped down the street, his hopes, his imagination in full blossom. Being on the streets was going to be fun! He'd have a great time. This was the life! It would be one big game from morning to night! Chinche constructed a picture in his mind of a romantic, carefree existence in which he would live for the moment, savouring life to the full, spending his money as soon as he got it. He'd become a millionaire, have a house made of candy with fountains gushing lemonade . . . or maybe coke, or . . .

Strays

Twin beams of light stabbed the darkness behind them. The blazing headlamps of a car reached out. Angel and Angelina broke into a run, their long shadows flailing ahead. The car swept past and became a pair of diminishing red lights. They stopped running, bending double, breathing hard. Angel knew he'd made a mistake. He'd thought that, by walking to one of the quiet residential areas, they'd be safer, but all he'd achieved was to make them more conspicuous. A police car had stopped them. They'd been questioned, told not to show their faces around there again. Now he didn't know what to do. One thing was for sure, they weren't going back, ever—not after that last beating César had given him and . . . and the things he'd tried to do to Angelina. If only he was twelve instead of ten he'd punch César's face to pulp.

'Gatita's cold, Gatita's tired,' Angelina whined.

'Better keep going,' Angel gasped. 'You heard what that pig said to us.'

But neither of them moved. Slowly they sank to the ground, then crawled into a ditch, burrowing amongst the dry leaves. Angel put his arm round his sister, and she curled up defensively like a little wood-pooch, the kind they used to pretend were marbles when he was a child.

'Sh! Someone's coming!' Angel held his breath. Heavy, booted feet were tramping towards the ditch.

A panicky sob was starting up inside him. The footsteps drew level and stopped.

'Dios mío! Look what we've got here!'

A boot thudded into Angel's ribs. Angel yelped and risked a quick upward glance. Two men in paramilitary uniforms, sub-machine guns slung across their shoulders, stared down at him. Every hotel had its armed watchmen, every residential block its complement of vigilantes, hired from private security companies to patrol the area. A steel-shod heel ground into Angel's knee.

'Move on, filth! Here we like the streets kept clean.'

Angel knew it would be useless to look for a place to rest until they were clear of the residential area. If the vigilantes didn't get them, the pigs, la policia would. For kids like himself and Angelina they carried lengths of lead-filled hosepipe up their sleeves.

They walked for what seemed like hours, heading for La Olla, a district near the city centre where the prostitutes and drug pushers hung out: there, in the most dangerous part of the city, street kids could find a kind of safety in numbers.

A goods train wailed in the distance while they scurried across a dual carriageway, making a detour to avoid a gang lurking behind some trees near the traffic lights. Angel caught a glimpse of their 'big key', a sledgehammer for battering in the door or the windscreen of any car whose driver was foolish enough to stop just because the lights were red.

The distant skyscrapers of the city centre blushed in the dawn when, exhausted, they rested and waited beside the railway line. Hitching a ride shouldn't be too difficult: the passenger trains thundered past but the long goods trains laboured more slowly through the city, and this particular crossing was near the top of a hill. Angelina began snivelling again.

'I want Mama! I want Mama, I want— '

'You can't have her!' Angel shouted roughly because he wanted her too, but to go back? No, it was unthinkable.

'I'll tell you a story, shall I, Angelina?' he blurted out. He'd seen it on TV. 'The girl in the story is really you.' She leant her thin body against his.

'Is it really me, Angel? Is it really?'

Angel concentrated hard on the pictures he remembered of the ragged girl being magically transformed into a magnificently dressed lady, like the ladies he sometimes saw travelling to parties in enormous, shiny cars. He retold the story, decking his sister in fine silks and jewellery and helping her into a golden coach; and he was the handsome prince in the splendid palace with marble fountains and . . .

The shriek of the train's whistle broke the spell. The beautiful clothes became rags again and the pearls in her hair turned back to nits; amethysts around her neck once more became purple bruises.

A slow train rumbled and clanked by, so they perched on the footboard of one of the freight cars, holding on to the padlocked sliding doors. Every mile towards the city centre was a mile further from home, or what had been their home. Angel nurtured his resentment: it filled the wasteland inside him.

The train entered a crumbling canyon of eight-storey blocks. Rows of curtainless windows, bare light bulbs, exposed lives: a family quarrelling in a small room; an old man, naked except for a truss, squashing bugs on a wall; four children making paper flowers while a man and a woman copulate on a mattress behind them. Abruptly interposed between Angel and this human warren was a military train, halted in a siding with soldiers sitting upright in open cars, their helmets gleaming like beetles.

Angel took Angelina's hand, saying 'Come on, this is the goods-yard. We jump off here.'

They ducked under a stationary wagon, squeezed through a hole in a wire fence and entered the outer fringes of La Olla. Carrera Twenty marked the boundary line between the rich world and the poor world. On their side of this traffic artery, on the poor side, was *El Mercado de Los Ladrones*, the thieves' market which sold 'second hand' shoes, clothes, car parts, electrical goods, watches, jewellery. The shops were beginning to open up, the stall owners to unpack their goods, the street vendors to claim their patches and to lay out their wares on blankets. Angel and Angelina wandered down the mile looking for somewhere to sleep. On a concrete island, at a crossroads, four boys and a dog slept in a disorganised heap, their limbs entwined, oblivious to the growing volume of traffic.

Arm in arm they wandered into a little square in which an open market was being held. They pushed their way past piles of quartered red-fleshed watermelons, past strawberries which little boys kept free of dust by popping into their mouths and sucking, past stacks of cages containing songbirds which looked to be near to death, past open trays of tablets and pills, sold singly or by the handful. 'Sweeties for diarrohea'. Angel stopped beside a stall selling battered second-hand dolls. Vividly he saw the inside of their shack in the barrio, his mother . . . He dragged Angelina away.

'You're hurting me.'

'You'd think, wouldn't you, that the world would be overflowing with fucking dolls by now? I mean, they must make millions of them every year. What happens to them all?'

'I don't know. Maybe . . . maybe they get broken.'

'Or lost.'

'Perhaps people don't want them anymore or perhaps . . .'

'All right! No need to go on about it. It's not that interesting.'

Angelina tugged Angel's arm.

'Mira! Mira! Look at that kitten.'

She pointed at a thin white kitten, shivering in the middle of the pitted, cracked pavement, staggering on weak legs to avoid unheeding feet. Angelina bent towards it. The kitten looked up at her, walked towards her and climbed shakily onto her foot, butting its head against her hands. Gently Angelina lifted it, huddling her body over it as if shielding it against the world. Her expression was frightened, soft, vulnerable, changing to one of resentment, ready for the refusal, as she asked, 'Can I keep it? Oh please can I keep it?'

Angel shrugged. 'Why not?'

Angelina's face was like a flower just opened. 'He's so small and warm and he's mine. I didn't catch him. He came to me. He came into my arms all by himself.'

The kitten squirmed happily, purring loudly.

'What will you call it?' Angel asked. Angelina kissed the kitten.

'Gatita thinks she'll call him Huerfanito.' A tear fell on to Little Orphan's ear. Angelina buried her face in his fur. 'Angel, Gatita wants to know.'

'What?'

'Do you think Mama will come looking for us?'

Angel said nothing. The thought of Claudia desperately searching for them was too painful to bear. And then there was the other thought, the one he battled to keep at bay—that she might not come looking for them.

'Here, it's my turn to hold Huerfanito,' he said gruffly.

'Give him to me!'

'No, it's my cat, all mine. I'm the only one he loves. His love is for me and nobody else.'

They sat in the gutter, resting. A woman passed by carrying a tray of bananas. Angel looked up. There was something about the back of her head, her hair. Angel jumped up, his lips shaping to call out, 'Mama!' The woman turned. A stranger. He smacked his sister over the head, his voice harsh with pain. 'Well, don't just sit there drooling over that stupid animal!' And then a man pressed a coin into Angel's hand and walked on, not waiting to be thanked. Angel blinked away his tears.

'Ten pesos, Angelina! We can buy a whole bag of sweets!' They hurried to the nearest sweetie-stall, lingered over their purchase, then devoured the lot within a matter of minutes.

'Angel! Where's Huerfanito? Where is he? I put him down here . . . I just turned to reach for the sweets and . . .'

They searched along the gutter, in doorways, under the wheels of a parked car, calling the kitten's name.

'Where is he? Where is he?' Angelina screamed. 'Huerfanito, where are you? Why did you leave me? What's happened to you?'

They didn't find him.

Angel selected an empty piece of pavement outside the barred window of a jeweller's shop. From a stall nearby he begged an empty cardboard carton which they pushed close against the wall, below the window ledge and curled up inside. Shock, fear, pain, exhaustion exacted their toll. An old woman, dragging a sack which contained all her possessions, stopped beside the carton. Her face, even more wrinkled than her stockings, peered at the two sleeping children. She removed their shoes and popped them into her sack. Satisfied that they had nothing else worth taking, she shuffled on, leaving them to their twitching and moaning and stifled cries.

They slept through the bustling, busy day. Now and then people stopped to admire the valuables displayed in the window, the necklace of tear-shaped pearls, the blood-red rubies, the emerald crucifix. Others paused to look at the shining two-tone BMW inside a small compound beside the shop, protected from the public by a wire-mesh fence. No one gave a second glance at so common a sight as two urchins sleeping in the street, or even noticed the label on the carton: 'Fragile. Handle with care.'

Snow White

On the third floor of the delapidated warehouse, sunlight shafted through the narrow, barred windows of the large bare room. Seated at long wooden tables sixty boys worked in silence, assembling an edition of *The Pop-Up Book of Classic Fairy Tales*. On the table beside each boy was a pile of hard-covered books and stacks of pre-cut card, which were the pop-up pictures in their unfolded state. After only one morning at this work Nelsón's fingers were black with layers of dried glue. Fold the card here, here and here according to the dotted lines on the back, open each book at the correct double pages, glue tabs A, B and C onto the pages in the marked spaces, leave to dry, close and open the previous book to check that everything works properly, then on to the same picture in the next book.

After his father had been killed by the soldiers Nelsón had lost his job in the mine. You didn't keep a good job like that without someone there to look out for your interests, and with his father dead . . . fold the card, there, there and there, glue tabs A, B and C . . . there had been the rent to pay, his younger brothers and sisters to feed, the money lenders to keep sweet. For a lump sum his mother had signed a contract binding him to live and work in this place for three years.

One corner of the room had been sectioned off into a glass-fronted cubicle for El Capitán, their overseer. Inside the cubicle was an old wind-up gramophone. A badly scratched record crashed out martial music. To

Nelsón it sounded like the kind of music you heard on the radio when something serious had happened, like another government minister being bumped off by the guerillas—except that, on the radio, the music didn't go click, click, or jump several notes, or slowly grind to a halt. Under cover of the music Nelsón snatched a whispered conversation with the boy on his right.

'When do we eat?'

'Midday. When the hooter goes.'

'Jesus, some dump, eh?'

The boy, Rafael, shrugged. Nelsón turned to the boy on his other side. He was almost bald with the occasional whispy tuft of hair, his domed forehead wrinkled in a perpetual nervous frown. Every few seconds his hand twitched upwards, removing a stream of greenish snot from the scab-encrusted runnel between nose and lip, transferring it to the leg of his torn trousers.

'What's your name?'

'They call me Muñeco.'

'Been here long?'

Muñeco darted a frightened glance behind him, rolling his eyes in warning. Too late—Nelsón's body exploded with pain as something smashed into his spine. He let out a cry and half turned to find El Capitán standing over him, a thick knotted rope-end in his hand. He thrust it under Nelsón's nose, forcing his head back.

'No talking! And work faster! All of you—work faster!'

Nelsón concentrated fiercely on his task, trying to forget the glue fumes which made his eyes smart, trying to forget his throbbing back and everything that had happened in the last ten days. For the first time since being put to work this morning he lifted his mind beyond his misery, beyond the mechanical task he was performing and saw the picture he was making. It was part of some story, seven dwarves, underground. He looked more

closely and realised they were down a mine. Nelsón's
sharp intake of breath turned to choking sobs.

'It's the fucking glue!' he snarled in response to Rafael's
glance.

'That's not all it does to you,' Rafael muttered through
the side of his mouth. 'Take a look at Muñeco.' A spasm
of shaking had overtaken Muñeco, his head nodding up
and down. Rafael added, 'When you start to lose the
feeling in your fingers, or when you seem to be looking
at everything through smoked glass, then you'll know
it's time to get the hell out of here.'

A wolf jumped out of Muñeco's page, trying to break
down a shack in which three little pigs were hiding. The
whole bench trembled with Muñeco's shaking.

'For Christ's sake!' Rafael hissed. 'How can I glue this
fucking thing straight with you doing that!'

Muñeco's head nodded, frowning anxiously.

The hooter sounded for lunch. El Capitán unlocked
the big, iron-bound doors and let the workers down
the stairs into the yard. An old crone was filling bowls
from a garbage bin containing a fatty broth of scraps,
potato peel, bones, offal and nameless bits of gristle. It
smelt good.

Nelsón took a bowl and squatted on the ground.
Boys were sitting around smoking. The yard was the
only place they were allowed to smoke. Only a fool
would break that rule. With all that flammable glue
and other material a fire inside the locked workroom
didn't bear thinking about. Tobacco, grass, perica, Ma
Bruja, the old crone, supplied them all—at a price. And
the price of a smoke was obtained by satisfying the
sexual needs of certain of the men who worked in the
warehouse on the first two floors of the building—that
much Nelsón deduced for himself by observing couples
disappearing into corners and up stairways. The hooter
sounded again.

Fold, fold, fold, glue along the line, on and on. After what seemed hours and hours, with boys battling to keep their red, suppurating eyes open and being beaten if they failed, the final hooter of the day was heard. El Capitán fastened the wire-mesh shutters over the window of his cubicle and departed, leaving the boys locked in for the night.

The chanting of the ragged, half-starved assembly filled the locked room.

'Boys united never die young! Boys united never die young!'

Rows of old-young faces made a circle round Nelsón. He stood beneath the room's single bulb in an island of light. Pepe, the oldest boy there, held up his hand. There was instant silence except for the beating of moths' wings against the bulb.

'Let the entertainment begin!' he commanded. 'Come on, Nelsón, we all had to do it when we were new here!'

'What do you want me to do?'

'Sing, dance, tell a joke, anything. But if we don't like it, you get the thumbs down and have to pay a forfeit.'

The only song Nelsón could remember was a jingle for selling Coca Cola.

'I want to teach the world to sing in perfect harmony,' he sang, knowing that it was coming out as a flat tuneless drone.

'He sings like un gallito, like a cockerel with a sore throat!'

'Go on, be a cockerel, pretend you're a cockerel!'

'Un gallito! Un gallito!'

Nelsón capered and crowed and flapped his elbows, but one by one the thumbs went down, even Rafael's. A floorboard was lifted.

'Your forfeit,' Pepe said, 'Is a visit to the underworld. Down you go!'

Nelsón crawled into the space between the floor and

the ceiling of the warehouse below them. The loose board was replaced and someone stood on it so that Nelsón couldn't lift it. He lay on his side in a blackness that stank of fungi, rat droppings, dry rot and secret cobwebby smells. Something tickled his face. In his panic to brush it away he banged his elbow on a beam. Close to the back of his neck an invisible creature stirred and scuttled. Thud! Thud! Thud! A wild dance began a few inches above his head, feet thumping and stamping. Every bone in his body seemed to vibrate, his brain to turn to jelly. His hand encountered a hard, round shape—a skull. His hesitant exploration revealed that the skull was part of a whole skeleton, picked clean by the rats, no doubt. Cunning. If a boy died, they put him under here and claimed he'd run away. Not only was his disappearance explained, but his parents or whoever signed the contract then had to repay the lump sum. There'd be a nice little share out over that one. Nelsón shivered. Carlos Garcia, Paco Avarre, Jose Martine, boys from his barrio, all had been put into bonded labour and later reported as having run away. Like everyone else in the barrio, Nelsón had assumed they'd either joined a street gang, or gone to another barrio or left the city altogether.

'Boys united never die young! Boys united never die young!'

Thud! Thud! Thud!

Further ahead a gleam of light appeared. Someone had lifted a floorboard. Nelsón crawled towards the opening, squeezing head and shoulders between rough, splintery beams, scraping shins over sharp-edged joists. When he was nearly there the board was replaced with a thump, shutting out the light. Overhead, the dancing took on a renewed frenzy. Again a board was lifted. This time, someone called his name through the gap.

'I'm coming, I'm coming!' Nelsón panted. 'Don't close it. I'm coming.'

Again they slotted in the board and stood on it and danced over it before he could quite reach it. Nelsón knew that if he didn't play their game, let them have their sport, he'd never get out. At the fourth attempt, bruised all over, hands and knees full of splinters, he was allowed to emerge.

'My God, look at the state of his hair.'

'Look at his face.'

Pepe stood astride the gap so that Nelsón had to crawl between his legs. All those eyes staring at him, searching for any tears, for any sign of weakness. Pepe's legs closed, trapping Nelsón's head.

'Because I'm so kind-hearted,' Pepe laughed, 'I'm going to give you another chance to entertain us.'

Lying in the corner behind Nelsón was a discarded copy of *Classic Fairy Tales*—discarded because the colours on the pop-up pictures had all been printed out of alignment and the fact not noticed until it was too late. On an impulse, Nelsón picked up the book. Probably nobody else in the room could read either. It was worth the gamble.

He opened the book at random. Out of the pages sprang a beautiful girl with white, white skin and cheeks as rosy as blood and hair as black as ebony. Nelsón pretended to read, making up the story as he went along, slowly turning the pages, moving his finger from one word to the next, remembering not to go too fast and to frown and hesitate over the occasional word. It was easier than he expected. The story was quite obviously about the same kind of life he knew so well. This girl of seven or eight was forced to run away from her home because she was badly treated. She found work as a maid with seven dwarves . . . The barracking died down. They were listening. One or two looked uneasily at Pepe to see how he was reacting. Pepe, too, was listening.

'And the seven dwarves worked in the local mine . . .'

There were knowing nods from some of the boys. Who else but dwarves and children could work in seams and tunnels so narrow that no adult could get into them? Someone gave a loud laugh.

'Some broad, eh? Seven men every night!'

Pepe rounded on him. 'That's less than your mother has!' There were no interruptions after that.

'One day the old woman came to the dwarves' cabana to push some perica.'

'Sounds like old Ma Bruja.'

'Shhh . . .'

Nelson turned another page. The new picture showed the young girl lying in something like a glass tent. Standing nearby, gazing through the glass at her was a man dressed in all the latest top-price gear. It was obvious what had happened. Like so many of the girls in his barrio, this girl, too, had been forced into prostitution. Maybe she had lost her job with the dwarves or maybe there was no other way to pay for a drug habit she couldn't kick. He'd heard about the high-class putas on the Avenida de Los Andes, who sat in glass-fronted rooms. The man would be a gringo Americano, of course; they were mostly the ones who liked the girls of seven or eight. The story seemed to end happily.

'And the Americano was so pleased with the girl with the skin like snow and the red, red lips that he gave her jewels and fine clothes. And he visited The House of Pleasure whenever he flew into the city on business. And every time, without fail, he asked especially for her. As for the old woman, la policia got hold of her and tortured her, making her wear red-hot slippers of iron until she revealed who her suppliers were.'

Nelsón closed the book with a snap. Against the silence he could hear a train rattling by. Over the heads of his audience he saw, through a barred window, railway

carriages, like a series of brightly lit lantern slides, a magic
lantern showing fairy tales of a different kind, glimpses of
unattainable worlds—children with two parents, people
in expensive clothes, a restaurant car with table after
table of mouth-watering food. The train passed. And
the thumbs were going up. They were going up!

Pepe put his arm round Nelsón.

'Not bad! Not bad at all! And now all that remains to
be done for you to be accepted into our group is to smoke
the pipe of peace with us.'

The boys sat in a circle on the wooden floor, with
Nelsón on Pepe's right while someone removed the bulb
from its socket. A deep drone emanated from the circle
of boys. They linked arms, swaying slowly from side to
side. Pepe filled a clay pipe from a plastic pouch.

'Tonight we dance with La Blanca,' he said.

Normally, if the boys wanted a special lift, they
smoked a mixture of tobacco and bazuko. Being a
halfway stage in the refining of pure cocaine, bazuko was
rougher in taste and cheaper. Bazuko was La Morenita,
the little dark-skinned servant of La Blanca, the White
Lady, the Snow Queen. Pepe took the first drag on the
pipe, then passed it to his right. Nelsón received it, still
wet with saliva, and sucked on it. He held the smoke in
his mouth, rolling it round his tongue, along the inside
of his lips. He let a little go tingling up his nostrils, then
drew it back again. His head felt clear, the roof of his
mouth was a high, cool, echoing edifice like La Catedral
de la Gloriosa. Slowly he drew the smoke deep into his
lungs. All his aches and pains melted away, his misery,
his resentment, all melted away . . . and the flames . . .
so fascinating, the way they licked and curled around
the stacks of paper, the way they leapt and jumped and
roared, and the centre of the blaze, so intense that it was
a dazzling white.

Only in Small Doses

The puppeteer who emerged from his makeshift theatre was not what Chinche had expected. He stared at the thick torso on a wooden trolley, at the stumps ending just below the groin and the ill-fitting ginger wig made from some coarse synthetic material. The man's head was on a level with his own.

'Interesting, isn't it?' he said, hauling down the floating balloon which had been tethered to the stage. 'No, don't look away, it's the ones who do who— ' He gave a sharp laugh and, taking a block of wood in each hand, propelled his trolley up and down the sidewalk as he went about packing up his show. Chinche watched a glove puppet, whom he knew to be Ernesto, a simple peasant, helping Busca's left hand put the other puppets into a carpet-bag.

The play had been about a country ruled by animals. Chinche had laughed at the General, a hippopotamus with absurdly exaggerated gold epaulettes, and at the hyena in a pin-striped suit. It had taken his mind off his hunger and the panicky feeling that he didn't know when the next meal would be or where he would sleep.

'Busca is what they call me. It's short for Buscapleitos. Being only half a person, I'm only given half a name. And you? What do they call you?'

'Chinche.'

A growling voice came from deep within Busca's diaphragm.

'Grunni! Grunnaa! We could use a cute little kid like
him right now.'

'Who, me?' said Chinche. Busca's frog-like face split
into the semblance of a smile.

'My friend, Caciquismo the dragon, is reminding me I
need a lad to act as lookout and to collect the money, that
sort of thing. My last lad made the mistake of sleeping in
the gutter.'

'What do you mean?' Chinche asked, having done just
that for the past two nights. Busca stuffed the last of his
props into the carpet bag and manoeuvred his trolley to
face Chinche.

'My last lad? A street-cleaning machine mashed him
up. But there are worse dangers than that. Take my
advice—never, never sleep alone in the streets. Five is
a reasonably safe number, not less.' He outlined some
of the dangers: youngsters like Chinche kidnapped for
sexual purposes, for snuff movies, for blood banks and
for the 'spare parts' trade.

'What's that?'

'Hospitals and clinics willing to buy hearts, kidneys,
eyes, and no questions asked.' From the carpet-bag
Ernesto's rustic voice called out, 'Are you going to
offer him the job, or not?'

'Yes I am.'

'Well, do it then!'

'What do you say, you little thumbtack, do you want
the job? Can't offer you much—your food, somewhere
to sleep and a little extra maybe.'

'And good companions,' Ernesto added. 'Don't forget us.'

A huge grin spread over Chinche's impish face.
'Agreed!'

'Good!' cried Busca, clapping his two wooden blocks
together. 'You look as though you could do with
something inside you, so let's get going.'

Busca pushed himself through the streets of La Olla with Chinche beside him. Dangling from one stall were pairs of polystyrene legs wearing a variety of jeans. As Busca passed by, the amplifier boomed out: 'Hey hombre! People usually provide their own legs, but if you buy from us you can have the legs for free.' Busca hurled a friendly curse by way of reply, and with his arms working like pistons, pushed on past piles of fruit until he came to the sausage seller.

'Choose the one you want,' he said to Chinche.

Chinche chose a churingo, a thick garlic sausage, the kind with a smooth, tight skin which bursts and squirts savoury juices onto the roof of your mouth when you bite into it.

Busca shouted, 'Holá, Belin! Qué tal?'

A sewer-scavenger whose top half was protruding through a manhole in the sidewalk grinned at Busca and raised a hand in salute. The two torsos chatted while the rest of the world passed by.

They moved on. Busca told Chinche that he himself had spent a large part of his childhood on the street. He had run away from home, he said, for much the same reason as most did—because life was better on the street.

'Mama Calle, Mother Street, took care of me. I was never as hungry on the streets as I was in my barrio, not after I learned the tricks, not after I knew what was what and how many beans made five. But you . . .' He shook his head. 'The innocent don't last long on these streets.' Rivulets of sweat escaped from under Busca's stiff wig and ran down the side of his face. 'You push for a bit,' he grunted, and then: 'You should learn to beg.'

'Exactly.' chirped Ernesto who was now on the end of Busca's arm. 'You took the very words out of my mouth. You can't survive on the street unless you know how to beg.'

Busca's wig seemed to nod even more emphatically than his head.

'I couldn't have put it better myself.' He swivelled to catch Chinche's eye. 'There you are! If my right-hand man here says it's important, then it is. If we fall on hard times, or if you find yourself on your own for some reason, then begging is the thing for you. You don't know how lucky you are being small and defenceless. Once your voice breaks and the beginnings of a moustache appear on your lip, pity turns to hostility and— '

'Grunni, grunnaa!' groaned Caciquismo. 'Is this going to be another of his lectures?'

'You know what he's like,' replied Ernesto, bobbing up and down angrily. 'Ruins half our plays because he'll never learn that while the public enjoy a little taste of medicine, they don't want the whole bottle rammed down their throat.'

'Time you went back into the bag!' Busca snapped, plucking Ernesto off his hand and stuffing him into the carpet-bag.

'That's very offhand treatment!' Ernesto's muffled voice protested. 'You're the most manipulative person I know.'

'What you have to remember,' Busca said to Chinche as they trundled past a line of stationary tanks, 'is that begging is a business transaction.'

'What's that mean?' Chinche asked, his tongue exploring between his fingers for churingo grease. A heavy sigh escaped from the carpet-bag.

'He's trying to say that they give you money and, in return, you make them feel good about it.'

They were out of La Olla now, heading into a smarter area.

'Different audiences want different stories,' Busca was saying. 'The experienced street kid is an actor who— '

A woman was selling carnations. Chinche panicked: suppose he was captured and taken back to that awful place?

'Hey! Slow down, Chinche! This isn't a race!' Busca scratched his scalp by means of rubbing the coarse wig up and down on top of it. He began to curse and sweat even more profusely. Chinche wondered if his stumps were hurting him. Several stray dogs had knocked over a dustbin and were scavenging through the spilled contents.

'There's always that, of course. But only as a last resort. Push, boy! Push!'

Chinche learned, from an increasingly irritable Busca, of the hazards of taking stuff from a bin that was in territory controlled by one of the street gangs. You could be beaten up, disfigured, burned, even killed for doing that.

'This is Panther territory, by the way.'

In exchange for not hanging about the front entrance and begging from the hotel guests, the Panthers were granted first rights on the contents of the hotel garbage bins.

Through teeth gritted with pain, Busca said, 'When I was a kid we used to find the pickings were best when there was a conference on at a hotel. People are more wasteful when someone else is paying. Full bins and empty resolutions, that's conferences for you.' Busca stopped at some steps at the back of El Lujomercado, a well-known department store. Flopping off the trolley, he began to shuffle on his bottom up the steps. One look at his expression was enough to tell Chinche not to attempt to help him. 'If you must do something, carry the trolley,' Busca barked.

Once inside the rear entrance to the department store and back on his trolley, Busca nodded towards the folding iron gates and the empty elevator shaft beyond them.

'This is where I live.'

'What, down the bottom of the shaft?' Chinche said.

'No, in the elevator. It's not used at night.'

The red light on the panel registered 'Top Floor'. Busca slid his wooden hand blocks first under one buttock then under the other, chocking himself up so that he could reach the control button. The elevator arrived with a whine and a judder. Through the folding iron gate Chinche could see that it was filled with buckets, mops, garbage bins, empty cartons. Busca rattled the gates open and propelled himself in, followed by Chinche. Ernesto's head popped out of the carpet-bag.

'Living in an elevator: it has its ups and downs! But I'll have you know, this is the nerve centre of the nation, the hub of the universe.'

Busca seized Ernesto by the throat. 'That's enough cheek from you, you legless bastard.'

'Legless bastard yourself!'

'Puppet!'

'Puppet yourself!'

'And what's that supposed to mean, dummy?'

'It means that all your life you've been manipulated by other people, danced to someone else's tune and wha–aah!'

Busca squeezed Ernesto's throat till he was silent then pushed him back into the bag. Angrily he jerked his trolley round, cracking Chinche on the shins. Perspiring heavily, he snatched off his ginger wig. His scalp looked as if it had received a skin graft from a diseased toad. Chinche's gasp was clearly audible to Busca who gave an ironic bow.

'Yes indeed. A very eloquent comment. People are more offended by the sight of me than by what caused it.' He pulled out a glove puppet from his carpet-bag, a two-faced, double puppet. He turned one face towards Chinche. 'This is the sort of man who runs a big company.' He turned the puppet the other way. 'And this is a nineteenth-century slave driver. Look, see his whip at the ready.' Busca slipped his hand inside the glove, twisting it from one face to the other.

My name is Max Profit, Max Profit is my name;
You see how the two of us are one and the same.

He shook Max hard. 'I hate you!' he hissed, swaying sideways on his trolley, nearly overbalancing.' I used to work for IZC you know, International Zinc Corporation, the company that buys up all the ore from El Monton de Plata. A good, steady job maintaining the machinery.' Viciously Busca jabbed a finger through Max Profit's eye, piercing the papier mache skull. 'Well, one day I was so inconsiderate as to cause a hold-up in production. The ore crushers had to stop, just for the sake of my legs—what was left of them after they had been mangled between the rollers.'

Busca twisted one of the puppet's stuffed legs till it came off. So much anger frightened Chinche. Usually, when adults were angry it ended up with them hitting you. Rip! The other leg was torn from the body. Busca flung Max Profit to the ground and jerking the wheels of his trolley forward, crushed its skull. As he continued his story, Busca made furious runs at the elevator gates, bashing against them, backing off and bashing into them again.

'The whole thing,' Crash! 'Need never have happened if there'd been any safety precautions. But that would have been inconvenient.' Crash! 'And we wouldn't want to frighten away foreign companies, would we? I mean, what are my legs worth compared to that?' Crash! Crash!

Ernesto was out of the bag again.

'And so, my friends, having disposed of his legs, we come to the bald truth about his head.'

According to Ernesto, Busca's pitifully small compensation had soon disappeared in hospital bills. The doctors had been particularly keen to experiment with a new pain-killing drug for an American company before launching it in the USA. Crash! Unfortunately, they'd overestimated the amount that could safely be administered and there'd been several nasty side effects.

Ernesto peered closely at Busca's head.

'My God! Just looking at it makes me feel sick. I wouldn't touch it if I was paid a fortune. No wonder his wife ran away from him.' The puppet swivelled on the end of Busca's arm and faced Chinche. 'And that concludes this hair-raising little story!'

'I tried begging for a while,' Busca said, 'For kids it's not so bad, but when you're an adult, it's different. I discovered that what you get free costs too much.'

'That's right,' Ernesto said, 'the poor thing was in a real state until I took him in hand.'

The sweat was making Busca's shirt stick to his thick torso. He rolled himself a joint of marijuana and smoked it in silence, letting small puffs of smoke escape from his mouth and re-inhaling them through his nostrils. He regarded the little Indian boy through heavy-lidded eyes.

'Reality is a dangerous substance,' he said quietly, passing the joint to Chinche. 'It should be taken only in very small quantities by the young, only in very small doses.'

Chinche inhaled deeply. Busca nodded approvingly.

'Yes, reality, that's the killer.'

Sometime in the small hours of the morning Busca said, 'There isn't room in here for a dog to lie down. You can sleep on the elevator roof. You'll be safe up there. Safe from other people, I mean.'

Chinche climbed through the hatch and lay curled up in the darkness while, below, him, Busca filled the shaft with the voices of a dozen different puppets. The motor whined, steel hawsers hummed, draughts of stale air rushed over Chinche, a light flashed as they passed a floor. All night long Busca kept the elevator moving up and down, up and down, the voices winding through Chinche's dreams, panting, screaming, arguing—dreams in which Chinche was never sure whether the sensation of falling down a long dark shaft was merely a nightmare or some frightful reality.

Maggots

In the computer room of the University of the Andes, Carmen Helena gazed, unseeing, at the notice: 'No smoking. Smoke can damage these machines.' Her mind was on the topic of her thesis. It was important that she keep on the right side of her head of department. He was strong on Poverty. And Carmen Helena was not unaware of the fact that Third World poverty was selling well in North America and Europe. There were rich pickings to be had from Poverty. It was the 'in' topic at conferences.

After some thought she decided there might be decent mileage in the street kid as a topic. She always put 'the' in front of things when she wanted to sound impressive. 'The Street Kid: Trickster in Modern Garb?' or 'Hunters and Gatherers of the Urban Jungle'. Papa, of course, would have it typed by one of his secretaries and he had connections who could emboss the leather cover in gold lettering.

She turned off her computer, preparing to leave. The street sparrows, the fruit birds, the maggots—whatever name one gave them, they had definite possibilities. What she was after was weird rituals which could be compared with Amazon tribal customs; power structures and pecking orders that could interestingly be contrasted with those found in animal societies, or perhaps in a big business corporation; some clever observations on attitudes to ownership with, maybe, a neat little parallel between the street kid and a more primitive, pre-capitalist phase of society. She would go right now and visit that enthusiastic young priest who worked with the street kids . . . what was his name? Oh, yes, Paco. He had given one or two hard-hitting addresses to university audiences in which he had not shrunk from criticising the government for its lack of interest in the poor, a brave thing to do in these fraught times. There had been a collection afterwards for *El Sagrado*, the sanctuary which he ran, a place where kids could come in off the street.

The porter at the main gates of the university summoned a taxi for her, assuring her that the driver was known to him personally. Papa always insisted on this precaution. He said it wasn't worth the risk, getting into a taxi with a driver you knew nothing about, especially alone and certainly if you were a woman. Every week one heard stories of passengers who had been driven to some lonely backstreet and robbed by the waiting accomplices. Carmen Helena had never in her life walked in any of the city's streets, never more than a few metres from her car to a fashionable cafe or one of the classier shopping centres or stores. She travelled in a locked car from her father's house, with its barred windows and armed vigilantes patrolling the garden, to the next fortress held by the Haves against the Have-nots.

The taxi had been stuck in a long line of honking traffic for nearly ten minutes when a man pushing a handcart along the kerb drew level with them. In the cart was a dead body.

'Not another union boss!' joked the taxi driver, winding down his window. Carmen Helena kept her window firmly closed despite the heat.

'You know what they say,' replied the man, removing the cheap cigar from his mouth. 'The term of office for a union boss is short, because it's for life.' Even at a distance of several metres his poncho smelled of onions and dung and earth. 'My last stiff—it was the first job he'd had in fifteen years. There's some earn more dead than they ever did alive.' The man was resting on the shafts of his cart now. 'Do you know, I even had a stiff who voted at the last election. There were more votes than voters, that's for sure.'

Carmen Helena leaned forward and hissed to the taxi driver, 'Ask him what he's doing with that body.'

'Bless you señorita, there's a lively trade in stiffs, a lively trade! Let's see. There's your hospitals and medical schools and such like, that's your highest class of trade, of course. For the likes of me and him it's mostly, well . . . a wonderfully useful thing is your human body. The tendons, dried and powdered—that's your glue; the bones—your knife handles and the like; as for the blood, it— '

The taxi driver said, 'I thought horses and oxen were used for that sort of . . .'

'Oh, they are. But they're more for your big operator, your full-time men. For your small buyer without much capital, the occasional stiff is more suitable, cheaper, easier to come by in this city.' The man puffed at his cigar. 'Ever heard the saying, "two flies will eat a horse quicker than a lion?"'

'No.'

'Maggots, that's what it means. Flies breed maggots, millions of them. And maggots live off dead flesh. And do you know what you do with maggots?'

'No.'

'You sell them at a nice profit to poultry keepers. They give the poultry a special "gamey" flavour, so I'm told. Like I always say, there's a good living to be made out of death.'

The traffic started moving again.

'I hope we're not having chicken tonight,' Carmen

Helena said as they pulled away from the Maggoty-Man.

Twenty minutes later the taxi driver said, 'Here we are! You're lucky. Not many would take you right to the door of El Sagrado, not when it's in La Olla.'

Carmen Helena took the hint and tipped him double. She looked nervously up and down the dusty, pot-holed lane. People were staring at her curiously. She was glad she had taken the precaution of removing her jewellery and spectacles and of leaving her handbag behind. In the middle of a crumbling brick wall was a steel door. Carmen Helena knocked on it. The door opened a crack and a brown face peered out at waist height.

'I've come to see Paco.'

The door opened wider and the girl led Carmen Helena into an open yard surrounded by a high brick wall. Along one side of the yard were a couple of half-open cubicles housing primitive showers. Boys were playing football in the middle of the yard; another group was using an old bicycle with its handlebars reversed to play at toreadors. Several girls were sitting on the ground playing cards; one girl had a baby asleep on her lap.

Through a flutter of washing, Carmen Helena spotted Paco. He was in a corner, wearing boxing gloves, sparring with one of the bigger boys. He caught sight of Carmen Helena, took his eye off his opponent and was floored by a punch. A cheer went up. Paco got to his feet, grinning.

'OK. That's it for today. We have a visitor.'

He charged through the game of football towards Carmen Helena, robbed one of the bigger boys of the ball, passed it to a smaller boy and advanced upon her, dragging with him an earnest-looking young man with long hair knotted at the back. Paco extended a fist still

encased in a boxing glove. Laughing, he removed it and
shook her by the hand.

'Welcome to El Sagrado! This is Emiliano, my assistant. He volunteered himself about three months ago.'

Surrounded by a clamour of children, Paco gave her
a brief tour of the yard while she outlined the purpose
of her visit.

'What do they want?' she asked, as the children
pressed round her. 'Should I give them money?'

'No doubt they'd take it if you offered it, but what
they want is for you to put an arm round them, to hold
their hands. They want your warmth and love. Yes, the
money is easier, isn't it?'

To cover her confusion Carmen Helena pointed to
three tall, windowless buildings overlooking the yard.

'What are those things?'

'Silos. I watched them being filled up yesterday.
International agreement. Sugar in one, grain in another,
coffee in another. The harvest was too good this year. A
glut on the market would mean cheaper food, and— '

Emiliano, interrupted.

'They might as well be silos for nuclear rockets, they'll
kill almost as many people by the shortages and the high
prices they'll cause. The men in the shiny black cadillacs
who make decisions like that are no better than the war
criminals who sent millions to the gas chambers. They
feed off the rest of us, they— '

'Hey!' Paco laughed. 'I'm the one who's meant to
give sermons around here! How about showing Carmen
Helena the crèche where the girls can put their babies.'

Presently the games dwindled; benches were set out,
a pile of plastic bowls handed round. Rows of hungry
children waiting for their free bread and soup. Their
stench, their sores, their obvious physical deprivation
and maltreatment, she had steeled herself for. What she
hadn't been prepared for was their eyes, eyes such as she

had never looked into before. Eyes in faces closed and cynical and knowledgable beyond their years; eyes that trusted nothing and no one; eyes which could be blank and expressionless one moment and pleading with her the next, not for money or cigarettes—the mouths and hands did that—the eyes pleaded for she didn't know what. But these eyes had nothing to do with the kind of research she and her professor were interested in.

Satisfied that Emiliano had the meal under control, Paco turned to Carmen Helena.

'Street children, you say?' He produced a bag of jelly babies and offered her one.

'I carry these to give to los gusanos. Of all the names we give these tragic children, it's the ugliest—maggots. Yet it's the one I prefer, because even maggots can turn into creatures with wings.' Paco sucked his sweet and smiled ruefully. 'As for me, there are many who want to see my wings clipped. When I give food to the poor they call me a saint, when I ask why the poor have no food, they call me a communist.'

'I know a quote when I hear one. You should always acknowledge your sources.'

'Ah, there speaks the true academic. No doubt your thesis will be very impressive, with credit for every comma and full stop given to every publication that ever used these devices; and footnotes on every page longer than the actual text.'

Carmen Helena laughed.

'If it's alright with you I'd like to talk to some of the children and make a few notes.'

'Yes, by all means. After the meal is a good time, they're less restless then. And they're more likely to talk to you here than on the street. You see, Carmen Helena, they have a deep mistrust of adults, and with good reason. I hope, I pray, that at El Sagrado they are beginning to lower their defences and talk more freely about themselves. Not that you should believe everything they tell you. They still live in a fantasy world for much of the time, a lot of it drug-induced, of course.' He sighed and suddenly looked older. 'Drugs are a big problem. These children are easy prey for the pushers.'

When the meal was over she took some of the children aside and asked the questions she had prepared. She hoped that before too long they might even let her accompany them back to their street haunts and meet others of their gang. In the meantime her list of questions was a good start, providing background data and the basic information for her kinship diagrams. There was something she wanted to double-check with Paco. Pulling out her notepad, she approached him as he stood, whistle in hand, directing another game of football.

'Can you spare a minute, Paco?'

'Con buena gana . . . here, Emiliano, take the whistle and watch that rascal Miguel.'

With the game swirling round them, Carmen Helena explained her diagrams. The black triangles and circles were the boys and girls she'd questioned, the white triangles and circles represented their natural parents; the lightly shaded symbols were people cohabiting with either parent.

'Analysed on the university computer there might be some useful correlations to be found. And this— '

Paco stooped to retrieve the deflated ball as it scudded past, putting it to his mouth, his cheeks bulging, his head nodding to her to proceed.

'And this black triangle here is Boy C, the one I want to ask you— '

'Boy C, indeed!' Paco shouted, hurling the ball back to the waiting horde. 'He's got a name and flesh and blood and feelings, hasn't he? Is that what you see standing in this yard? Black triangles?'

The ball rocketed into the goal. The boys cheered. Paco glanced at the crucifix high on the wall of the yard. Taking the diagram from her he converted the black triangle into a stick drawing of a priest in a black cassock, with a sour, turned down mouth.

'Sometimes I squawk too much, even for a black crow. You do your thesis whatever way you think best. Do you say your prayers?'

'Not recently. I mean, I— '

'Carmen Helena, I want you to take one of these children home with you tonight.' He saw the expression on her face and laughed. 'Don't worry, I don't mean literally. I wouldn't be doing the child any favours by suggesting that. No, I want you to take one of them home in your heart and in your thoughts. A child with a name, not an abstract problem. When you're having a meal, ask yourself what that child will be eating; when you are safe in bed, ask yourself where that child will be—that will be a kind of prayer, a prayer for these little maggots who scavenge out of the dustbins and off the dumps.' He looked into her eyes. 'These kids . . . they eat right through your defences. They've changed my life and if you're the person I think you really are, they'll change you.'

Even the Birds

Like a small rodent on its own and in the open, Nelsón dodged from shadow to shadow, searching for a place to sleep. He had been one of the few survivors from the fire at the factory. Sixty boys locked into a room three stories up. He had escaped by going under the floorboards. His hair was singed, the right side of his face scorched and the palm of his left hand was one big blister. His hand needed treatment, but hospitals were risky places: they asked dangerous questions like your name and address and wrote down details which could end up in someone taking him back to his barrio or to another factory because his mother had signed a legal document promising his labour. And the next place might be just as bad or even worse. He'd take his chances on the street.

The trouble was all the best places to sleep were already occupied—the warm grilles above basement bakeries, the vestibules of the larger shops, the spaces behind the pavement kiosks, the corners of the small junkyards. The prowling cars, the watching men, the gangs hanging around the food stalls, any or all of them might be a predator. He hastened towards the porch of a shop, only to find it occupied. Two boys inside a black, polythene disposal bag stared at him with dope-glazed eyes. Only their heads, covered by woolly caps, were visible but from their stubbly chins and moustaches he knew he would be no match for them. He moved on. Where could he go? If he stepped from the shadows on

to the edge of the kerb, before long a car would stop
and a door would open and . . . and there would be a
comfy seat and maybe a soft bed in a hotel room and
. . . Forget it—to put yourself in the power of any adult
was a mistake.

Keeping in the shadows, Nelsón sidled past a heap of
still-warm ashes into which two boys had burrowed.
They slept in each other's arms, two brothers by the look
of them, younger than himself. One of them clutched a
baby's bottle, half-filled with dark red liquid. Nelsón
eased it from the hand and walked rapidly on till he
came to an empty bench near the river.

Lovers were strolling by, arm in arm; the prostitutes,
who had come out with the stars, were parading their
beats; on the ledges of the buildings and in the trees
parakeets were selecting their final perch for the night.
A man with a guitar and a hat at his feet was playing
a tune which flowed whispering through the night like
the river behind him, a river floating garbage, dead dogs,
the occasional corpse. Putting the rubber teat to his lips
Nelsón tasted the thick, syrupy cough mixture. He
settled himself on the bench sucking, sucking, rocking
to and fro, comforting himself with the teat.

'Better move before the police find you here,' the man
with the guitar said. 'They don't like people sleeping out
in this part of town. Too near the tourist bits.'

His wanderings took him to the gates of the Park of
Heavenly Peace. He climbed them, negotiated the spikes
at the top and dropped to the ground. He'd had to use
his left hand and it was throbbing painfully. He walked,
whistling nervously, between rows of stone tombs and
sepulchres which looked like miniature palaces. Stone
slabs grated to one side. The tombs opened. Figures rose
out of them, surrounding Nelsón.

'Menearte!' said one of them. 'You only get to sleep
here if you're in the Boliverano gang.'

'Or if you're dead.' said Nelsón, trying to stop his voice shaking.

'You'll be dead if you don't get out of here! Go on, fuck off!'

At length he stopped at an all-night soup stall. Its patrons stood silently around, cocooned in their own misery: a black man, old before his time, twitching for his next snort of cocaine and not knowing where he was going to get it; an old woman who had forgotten her name; a stray dog which had torn open a garbage bag and was spreading the contents over the pavement; an ageing prostitute. The occasional car whizzed past, moving at a speed made impossible by day when the buses choked the streets.

The old woman lit a small fire in the gutter, gleaning her fuel from the scattered garbage: a tiny scrap of linoleum, bits of cardboard or plastic, shreds of oily rags. For kindling she used fallen leaves and dried orange peel which flared and popped and induced a wreath of smoke from the little heap. The others gathered round.

'On your own, sonny?' the prostitute asked. 'That's a nasty blister on your hand.'

Nelsón tried to blink away the tears. How was it that a simple, kindly question could hurt more than a curse or a kick?

'Jesus, these high heels are killing me!' she complained. 'Want to tell me about it, sonny?'

Out tumbled the story of his father being murdered by the death squad, of being sold into bonded labour to the factory, the fire, his first few disastrous days on the street. The prostitute bought him a cup of soup. Nelsón sat on the pavement, sipping it slowly. When it was finished he'd have to decide what to do and he couldn't think of anything. He felt himself falling sideways, the cup beginning to slip from his grasp. He jerked awake. The cocaine addict sweated and moaned.

'I suppose you could try La Casa del Nuevo Comenzo,' said the prostitute, placing a hand on Nelsón's shoulder.

'Where?'

'You know, it's one of those places where you're done good to. It's across the street from that place where they recycle old bottles. Jesus, these heels are killing me!'

A station wagon drew up at the kerb. The prostitute arranged herself for inspection. Two men in clean but simple clothes got out. One of them was dressed as a priest.

'Buenas tardes,' they greeted the company and made some joke about saying 'good evening' at two in the morning. They bought cups of soup and offered them all round. Nelsón took one. He didn't trust the men, but he wasn't going to refuse anything that was free.

'Gracias, señor.'

'My name is Emiliano,' said the younger of the men.

'And I'm Paco,' said the other, who wore the black cassock. Paco turned and said quietly to his companion, 'The foxes have holes and the birds have nests, but the son of man has nowhere to lay his head.'

Emiliano looked at Nelsón's face and hand and then went to the station wagon, returning with a first-aid kit. He applied salve and a bandage to the burned hand and offered Nelsón a pill for the pain. Nelsón took it but hesitated, doubtful. Supposing it was doctored? Paco popped one into his own mouth, swallowed, then opened his mouth and wagged his tongue at Nelsón.

'Well, must be off now,' he said to the company at large. 'Good luck and God bless you!'

Once the station wagon was out of sight, Nelsón swallowed his pill. He thought he might as well check out the place the prostitute had mentioned. Wearily he stood up to go.

Wedged among the top branches of the tree which overlooked La Casa del Nuevo Comienzo, Nelsón found he could look through a window into a dormitory lit by night lights which glowed in neat rows along both walls. Down each side of the room were twelve beds, each with a small girl asleep in it, each clutching an identical doll in a blue dress; all the beds had identical tartan blankets and identical chairs beside them on which towels were folded in an identical manner. It was a frightening sight. Even from the outside looking in, Nelsón felt a sense of panic, of suffocation, like a wild horse experiencing a bit and saddle for the first time.

He scrambled out of the tree and scurried on down the road till he came to the wide steps of El Museo del Oro. The portico was supported by pillars and behind some of these, people were sleeping: a young woman with a baby, an old man nursing a bottle of wine, two children no more than four or five years old, other shapeless bundles whose sex or age he couldn't make out. There was definitely safety in numbers. In a group you weren't so conspicuous, there was less chance of being singled out. He tried squeezing in next to the children, but a woman of terrifying aspect seized him by the collar and flung him down the steps. He sat there nursing his injured hand, looking at a poster on a pillar advertising the current exhibition in the museum—something about primitive man. He looked longingly at the pictures of the little straw huts inside their thorn barricades. They seemed so cosy and protected. But after twenty minutes, simply wandering about was better than sitting on the cold stone in the raw night air.

At last, in a weed-infested corner of a soap factory, Nelsón found a disused pan or tank where, in the past, brews of fats and caustic soda had boiled. Now, stripped of its zinc lining, the crumbling brick construction had become the factory's tip for corroding barrels which seeped acid and chemical waste. Beneath the pan was a furnace. Nelsón paused outside its small oval opening. Dawn was bringing a yellow glow to the heaps of animal fat and tallow at the side of the factory and revealed a multitude of feeding rats. Men were shovelling coal into furnaces below the soap pans. On the platforms above, women were coughing and choking on the fumes as they stirred and skimmed the pungent bubbling mixture. Beyond the coal piles large delivery vans were revving up, each one painted in fresh, clean shades of green, amidst which a beautiful smooth-skinned goddess ecstatically caressed a bar of the perfumed soap. Crawling into the old furnace Nelsón curled up and fell asleep.

Superman

'Que suerte! What luck!' Chinche kept exclaiming as he crouched behind a dustbin, putting on the blue tunic with the red 'S' on the chest, and the yellow and red shorts. 'Que suerte!' If he'd been any bigger he wouldn't have got into this suit made for a six-year-old. This rich kid, smelling of soap and clutching its mother's hand had walked out of the department store with a parcel under its arm. It had been child's play to snatch the parcel from the stupid bobo and run. Under the wrapping was a box and inside the box—a Superman outfit! It had been a good start to his free day. Busca's stumps were troubling him too much to operate the puppet theatre, so Chinche and the puppets had been given a day off.

Superman strutted down one of the fashionable shopping avenues receiving what he imagined to be admiring glances. He hovered at the window of a TV shop. The popular serial of Robin Hood was on. It was set in some foreign country, he couldn't remember which but, like in his own country, the guerilla forces seemed to have taken to the forests. Next, he paused on the fringes of an open-air restaurant. People sat at round tables under gaily coloured umbrellas. All those knives and forks! He'd been to an eating house once, a place where you either brought your own implements or ate with your fingers. Plates of food kept passing by. Caramba! It certainly looked good. Then Chinche realised these were the leftovers, what they scraped off the plates

75

into the bin. A waiter put a basket of bread rolls on a
nearby table. The couple broke open the crisp exteriors
and sank their fingers into them. Chinche wondered if he
could steal one without anyone seeing. Being Superman,
he discovered, had certain drawbacks, like having no
pockets for hiding things in.

He wandered into the Plaza de Bolívar with its
vast paved pedestrian precinct surrounded by impressive buildings. Sitting on a bench was an overweight
middle-aged man studying a colourful brochure filled
with pictures of folk dancers in splendid costumes and
golden beaches occupied by smiling people with golden
tans. The man was wearing a wide-brimmed cowboy
hat. Obviously a gringo Americano. Chinche smiled
winningly at the man and pointed to the brochure.

'It looks like a truly beautiful country, señor. Is that
where you come from? Is that your country, señor?'

'It's here, child,' he said in fractured Spanish. 'It's this
country, your own country.'

'Oh, I didn't recognise it.'

The man returned to his brochure and, waving an arm
around the plaza, read out in an accent that produced
strange throttled sounds from Chinche:

'The Plaza de Bolívar and its environs is a breathtaking
creation in steel, concrete and glass, which reflects the
civilised face of modern South America . . .'

The gringo broke off and consulted his phrase-book
before turning to Chinche and asking him if he wanted
to earn some money by being photographed. Superman in flight past the United Sugar Corporation building; Superman, by a trick of perspective, holding an
armoured car above his head—an American armoured
car, as the man proudly pointed out.

'OK, kid. That's all, muchas gracias.'

After some rather complicated undressing, the norte-
americano arrived at a money belt around his waist and

produced from it a crisp new note which he handed to Chinche. As the man disappeared into the crowd, Chinche slowly, disbelievingly unfolded the note. It couldn't be. It was! A five thousand pesos note, the largest denomination he had ever held in his hand. Five thousand pesos! Chinche bolted out of the square before the gringo could discover his mistake.

Westerns had become Chinche's great passion. Whenever he had a spare coin or two, which wasn't often, he spent it at the cinema. Sometimes he could duck through the turnstile without being seen, but usually they were wise to that dodge; and to the one where you walked through, pointing to the man behind you, saying, 'My dad's paying.' Chinche liked the films where the US cavalry came to the rescue and wiped out the Indians. So, it was to the Aztec Cinema that Chinche headed with his windfall. He calculated that, if he wanted, he could see 'Golden Spurs' several thousand times. Probably fifteen or twenty times would be enough, though.

Chinche came out after seeing the film only twice because he had a sudden hankering to visit a particularly splendid ice cream parlour against whose window he'd pressed his nose many a time. On the way there he passed a shop window in which was an open box containing a magnificent selection of felt pens. He hesitated. He'd been turned out of shops before. This time though, his dirty face and strange costume seemed to be invisible behind his money. Then came the satisfaction of pulling the caps off the fat tubes; the smoothness with which the moist tips ran across the glassy expanses of the shop windows, trailing all the colours of the rainbow behind them. And the joy of feeling the soft felt nibs flow across the polished surface of the white cadillac.

'What do you think you're up to?' a woman shouted. 'What are you doing to my car?'

She was plump and smelled strongly of perfume. She was obviously one of *la buena gente*, the people who never carried their own groceries, or washed their own cars, or cleaned their own houses. She lunged at him, causing him to drop the box.

Leaving the pens scattered on the sidewalk, Superman ran into an amusement arcade, skipping past lines of computer games, each offering a different way of annihilating the world—'Thermonuclear Armageddon', 'Star Wars', 'Last Battle of the Continents'—stopping finally at a pinball machine. Before one metal ball had negotiated the obstacles and settled in a scoring-pen, or disappeared down the slot at the bottom, Chinche was sending the next one on its way.

'Three million! Wow! I scored three million!' The lowest score possible started at one million.

Superman lifted a hotel in one hand and held it up. One of the Monopoly players at the pavement cafe, the Cafe Ludo, took the fallen piece and replaced it on the board.

'Thanks, kid.'

'Hey, Superman! You're good at rescuing people. See if you can get me out of gaol. I need a double six. Throw my dice for me!'

The dice spilled from Chinche's hand onto the board. The young man groaned and gave Chinche a playful cuff over the head. Not sure whether it was a joke or not, Chinche sidled away till the throng swallowed him up.

Chinche the big spender, the macho figure with the power and the money, the devil-may-care man-about-town, marched into the ice cream parlour. He seated himself beside the window. The proprietor approached, hostile, disapproving, ready to shoo him away. Chinche fanned himself with his paper money and said grandly, 'Here, take this and keep the ice cream and cokes coming until I tell you to stop.'

Chinche attacked a triple-headed cone, each head piled
with three different flavours, his face smeared with
vanilla, orange, strawberry, peppermint and chocolate.
He devoured his treat with an earnest expression on
his face, set on finishing it before it could be wrested
from him or somehow melt away, always demanding
that the next round be put in front of him before he'd
finished what he had. Three small, hungry faces pressed
against the glass, looking in at him, wide-eyed. With
magnanimous sweeps of his arm Superman motioned
them in.

'Come in, mis muchachos! Come in! Ices and coke on me!' He snapped his fingers. 'Camarero! The same again, and this time include my friends!' Forty minutes later, Chinche said, 'That's it all spent.'

'We have to be going now,' said one of the three small boys. The proud benefactor stood erect on the steps outside the parlour until his three guests turned a corner. Then he was sick.

Chinche was still staring regretfully at the pool of sick, trying to identify the individual flavours, when he noticed a boy of his own size staring admiringly at his Superman outfit. Being Superman, Chinche realised, made you too conspicuous if you wanted to snaffle something off a stall; and Busca liked him to dress beneath his proper station when taking the collection at performances, even to go barefoot. The outfit was, he had to admit, a little grubbier than when it had emerged from its box—felt pen streaks, the odd grease spot, ice cream and vomit here and there, a tear or two—but, on the whole it was still pretty smart.

'Swap clothes with you, if you like,' Chinche said.

'It's a deal!'

They undressed, watching each other warily. There were cigarette burns on the boy's protruding ribs.

'You hand your clothes over first,' Chinche said.

'No. You first!'

'Both at the same time, then. And don't try anything funny!' After several last-second snatchings away of the proffered items, the transaction was successfully completed. Chinche slid into the still-warm clothes.

'Your turn to save the world,' he said. 'I've got serious work to do.'

Simple Economics

Every time Angel stooped to retrieve a cigarette butt from the gutter, black and white dots buzzed before his eyes. On the other side of the street, Angelina too was scavenging for fag-ends. Between them they were lucky if they could collect half a kilo of tobacco in a day. It was the minimum amount the dealer in La Olla would accept. For half a kilo he paid out just enough for each to buy a bowl of rice and beans. Angel swooped on a lipstick-smeared butt. A good one. Women seemed to discard theirs sooner than men. His clothes chafed against the sores which had broken out all over his body. Fighting off the dizziness and the nausea he called to his sister, signalling that it was time for the early afternoon sports news. People would be gathering round the window of the television shop in the next street, producing a good crop of colillas. While Angelina went to collect their droppings, Angel moved to another of his strategic points, a bus stop.

A group of schoolboys stood at the bus stop. They wore the blue uniforms of the John F. Kennedy School and carried expensive-looking bags full of books. No doubt they were waiting for the school's own mini-bus. Boys like that didn't travel on city buses. To the boys of the John F. Kennedy School, the tattered, street-sparrow collecting collilas was invisible. They looked through him and past him. They were complaining loudly to each other about the amount of homework they'd been given. They were particularly vociferous about a 'problem' they

had been set. If it takes 4½ hours to fill a swimming pool
30 m by 10 m to a depth of ½m, how long will it take
to fill a pool twice as wide to a depth of 3 m?

'About two months if Gregor's gardener does it,'
proclaimed one of the boys. 'He's always behind the
bushes with the maid!' They all laughed. Angel stooped
for a filter-tip. He wished he had problems like that. The
boy called Gregor aimed a friendly blow with his bag at
a companion. A book tumbled out.

'Standard V Economics!' exclaimed the other boy in
disgust, kicking it out of Gregor's reach. 'That's simple
stuff! And boring, dead boring!'

The sun had set two hours since and still Angelina and
Angel had not collected enough tobacco to make up the
half kilo.

'Things will pick up soon,' Angel said, hoping to bring
a smile to Angelina's drawn face. The late night cinema
crowds, the groups hanging around the strip joints—all
these would yield their crop of fag-ends, but too late for
them to have any hope of eating until the early hours of
the morning. They argued about whether to deplete their
already inadequate store of tobacco by rolling themselves
a cigarette. It had been a long time since they had eaten.
If you inhaled really deeply it seemed to stop the hunger
and all the other aches and pains and make you feel less
tired. They weighed up the loss of tobacco against the
gain in being able to keep going with the collecting. They
rolled the cigarette and lit up.

At length they had the half kilo, but the dealer was four
miles away and they had no money for the bus fare. If
they walked it would be at least another hour before they
had money to buy a meal. If they stole a bus ride they'd
be there in less than fifteen minutes. But, if they were
caught . . .

'We'll walk,' Angel said.

'But Gatita says she's tired.'

'Fuck Gatita, we'll walk!'

Angel had heard too many stories about what the police did to you in those places where they took you for it to be worth the risk.

They dragged their weary legs through the streets, stopping once at a fountain for a drink, but resisting the temptation to join the crowd at the scene of an accident. People were going through the dying man's pockets, not just to take his money but also to find out where he worked and be the first there to claim his job.

The tobacco dealer placed the small brass piece on the pyramid of weights. The scales trembled in equilibrium, reflecting the light of the kerosene lamp hanging from the side of his stall.

'Exactly point five-eight of a kilo. Here you are, here's your money.'

Angel counted it, making a calculation in his head with a speed the boys of the John F. Kennedy School would have envied.

'But señor, this is not correct. We are nineteen pesos short. You have not paid us the full amount.'

The man shrugged. 'I know, but what else can I do? The price of food up, taxes up, even the cost of an honest bribe's gone up.' He pressed the tobacco into a wooden box. 'So what can a man do? Either he puts up the price of what he's selling, or he lowers the rate at which he buys.'

'But not by this much, señor! It's not worth collecting the stuff at this price.'

'There'll be others only too glad to accept that price, believe you me. Take it or leave it.'

Angel looked at Angelina.

'We'll take it,' he muttered. It was always the same. The less you had the worse you got out of any deal. You didn't have the reserves to sit it out and wait for prices to get better; and, if turning down a deal meant having no money at all and you hadn't eaten in a long while, it was hard not to take whatever was offered. On the nearby stalls all the food had gone up in price. Everybody, it seemed, could charge more, except themselves; they ended up with less.

That night, curled up in their cardboard box, they made a decision. Collecting collilas was no longer worth it. They'd try the car-wash business. It would mean going quite far out into the suburbs to find an area not controlled by one of the street gangs, but it was worth a try.

Setting up in the car-wash business wasn't as easy as they thought. Not having enough money to purchase even the basic plastic bucket, they'd tried to steal one. Buckets, however, have handles through which a chain can be threaded, and they're the kind of thing that's kept at the back of a stall or shop. In the end they'd had to hire one, handing over a deposit which left them penniless. Soon they'd paid out more for hiring the bucket than it would have cost to buy it, but they could never accumulate enough money to own it outright. Then there was the 'tax' levied by the policemen who lounged on the corner of the block where they operated. Without the goodwill of la policia they were lost. It was simply a practicality of survival to hand over half their earnings to them. The alternative was not to be allowed to earn anything at all.

After their dues were paid, they were lucky if they had enough to buy more than a couple of stale rolls. A stone mason let them sleep at night in an empty dog kennel in his yard. They slept surrounded by a regiment of stone angels, a regiment in which the baby angels outnumbered the others by ten to one.

Their patch was the traffic lights on the corner of the block. They were the only car-washers at the lights, but they had to compete for the drivers' attention with a blind seller of lottery tickets, a kebab vendor and a newspaper boy named Zurdo. If a person wound down a window for any one of these things, the chances were they'd buy something else as well. There were three minutes between the red and the green light. Three minutes in which to find a willing customer, wash and dry the windscreen and collect the money. It was hard work and if you hadn't eaten for a long time you were sometimes a bit slow and then the car would roar off on the green light without paying you. The bucket could do four windscreens, then Angel and Angelina had to walk the two-hundred metres to the stone mason's yard, refill the bucket and stagger back with it. One afternoon, tired and hungry, Angel had not moved fast enough and the toes of his left foot were badly pinched and bruised under a wheel. In the days which followed he and Angelina came close to starvation as Angel's painful foot slowed down their already decreasing rate of work, which meant they earned less, which meant they ate less, which meant they worked even slower.

It was the hour of the day when the traffic dwindled to no more than two or three at the red. They always tried the women first.

'Wash your windscreen, señora?' Angelina wheedled.

The woman looked the other way. They washed it all the same in the hope of a tip, which they didn't get. At the next red it was a lorry. They didn't bother with lorries—not enough time, and lorry drivers usually had hordes of their own kids to do that sort of thing. Then there was a Renault 21 and a driver who had no change. Angel limped back to the sidewalk.

'Gatita is hungry,' Angelina whimpered.

'I know.' Standing so close to the tantalising smell of the kebabs was a kind of torture. So far, Angel's daily barrage of hints had fallen on deaf ears.

'Government negotiates new loan with World Bank!'

Zurdo shouted. 'Read all about it!' He had different headlines for different types of cars. 'Bank robbery in city!'

The blind seller of lottery tickets gave a cynical laugh.

'It's the banks which rob us!'

He sat on the pavement, knees drawn up. Blue, white and pink tickets were pinned in overlapping rows to his jacket, making him look like some exotic bird. Dark glasses hid his eyes.

'Do you ever buy tickets yourself?' Angelina asked him.

'Not any more.'

'Government negotiates new loan with World Bank!'

'Zurdo, could I borrow a fag off you?' Angel asked.

'I lend you one today, you pay me back two tomorrow.'

'What if I can't?'

'Then you pay me back three the next day.'

Angel hesitated. They needed something to stave off the hunger pangs. Zurdo smiled broadly.

'You have nothing, so I help you, no?'

'Help me? Repaying you three times as much as you give me, that's helping me?'

Zurdo shrugged. 'That's business.'

There came the night when they had to choose between buying food or saving enough to hire the bucket again the next morning. That was the night on which the stone mason acquired a guard dog.

'Sorry, but I need the kennel now.' he told them. 'I've worked it out. It's quite simple, really. Too many of my angels are disappearing in the night, especially the small ones. The dog will cost less than my losses in angels. No hard feelings, it's just a matter of economics.'

Independence Day

The detention centre was like a large stone-floored cell, with cage bars at one end and across the top. Thirty-two children had spent the night there, with nothing to lie on and no blankets. At five-thirty in the morning a warden had appeared on the parapet and hosed them down with ice-cold water. Wet and shivering, Nelsón crouched in a corner next to a boy called Zurdo whose left eye was the colour of a sunset seen through the smoke of the IZC smelter. At least they hadn't been selected for the 'overflow' to be sent to the men's gaol. They all knew what that meant. Supplying children to the sex-starved prisoners was a profitable racket. They had been locked up because it was Independence Day, the 175th anniversary of the final breaking of the bonds of colonial rule. Events like that attracted attention. Press cameras and street kids were a recipe for bad publicity. So they had been rounded up and tidied away out of sight.

Not for the first time Nelsón and Zurdo wondered what was going to happen to them. When the Pope had visited the city there'd been a similar round-up. Many of the kids had never been seen again.

'Maybe they'll force us to work on the State Farm,' Zurdo said.

'Better than ending up dead in a ditch,' Nelsón replied, through chattering teeth.

On the other side of the iron bars a warden sat with his back to them, watching television and drinking coffee.

Even in his present predicament the coloured, moving
pictures had Nelsón pressing his face to the bars. The
film, which had been made specially for Independence
Day, was about the campaigns of the Great Libera-
tor, Simon Bolívar and how his ragged army, often
using guerrilla tactics against superior numbers, finally
defeated their oppressors.

'That's the riot police they're using for the cavalry,'
Zurdo said. 'They're the only ones with horses'.

The advertisements came on. Ice cream, Coca Cola,
Ford cars, North American pharmaceuticals, a trailer for
'Dallas'. The warden stood up and rattled the bars with
his baton.

'Out! Out!' he yelled, unlocking the door. 'Down that
corridor—move!'

Two windowless vans were backed up to the end of
the corridor, their rear doors open. Blows, kicks, violent
shoves; the van doors slamming and being locked; a slow
crawl through traffic; squashed together in the dark,
suffocating metal box, not knowing where they were
going. The radio was on in the front cab, a commentary
on El Presidente's motorcade which was approaching
the international football stadium and the assembled
masses. Nelsón put his eye to a small rust-hole in the
side of the van. They were passing the huge municipal
garbage dump. El Presidente would have passed this
way only twenty minutes earlier. Nelsón had met a
couple of kids from gangs living more or less permanently on the dump, surviving on what they could
scavenge. Rows of advertising boards had been erected,
completely hiding the dump from view. Yesterday you
could have seen *los basureros*, as they called themselves,
competing with the vultures; today he was treated to
a glossy panorama of the ideal life—a goddess of the
screen telling you how to stay slim, sizzling sausages
ten foot long and—

From the stadium came a quarter of a million voices raised in a well-drilled spontaneous outburst.

'Viva El Presidente! Viva El Presidente!'

The van resumed its crawl through the traffic, then turning off, began to speed up. Then the world exploded.

Nelsón opened his eyes. His arm was stiff and there was blood on his hand. He explored his head with his fingers, expecting to find his brains hanging out. Nothing. Slowly he sat up. He was on a grass verge, beside a corrugated iron fence across which was scrawled the slogan: 'If Justice is blind, she is also deaf and dumb and has a wooden leg.' The upturned van lay in a ditch, its radio at full volume. The two uniformed wardens were still in the cab, dead or unconscious.

Nelsón wasn't sure what had happened—whether it had been an FLN bomb or just a crash. He climbed painfully to his feet. The back doors had burst open. He could see three boys and a girl lying very still, in unnatural positions, inside the van. One of them was Zurdo. Of the others there was no sign. The radio was blaring out the national anthem:

> In freedom from the yoke of foreign rule we sing.
> And over mountain, forest, lake and plain shall ring
> The joyous voices of our children . . .

A train rumbled past, a military train, bringing into the city armoured cars equipped with machine-guns and water-cannon. Moving as fast as his shocked body would allow, Nelsón squeezed through a hole in the fence. One of the good things about this city was that it could swallow you up without so much as a burp.

The Gamin Look

Taking a deep breath, and clutching her bag tightly under her arm, Carmen Helena jumped on to a battered, garishly painted micro, one of the city's thousands of small, privately-owned buses. Until this moment she had never been on a bus, literally never rubbed shoulders with anyone outside her own rich little circle. Buses were nasty, dangerous things where you were bound to get your pockets picked, your bottom pinched, and where you'd almost certainly catch some horrible disease, or be offered drugged sweets by plausible strangers—this was what the nuns and her mother had impressed upon her.

But the words of Paco the priest still rankled. What did she know of the poor? he had asked. Once, when she was eight, she had been a stable lad in a Nativity Play. She had worn a pair of her father's striped pyjamas, freshly laundered; and her mother had made her look suitably dirty by smearing her face with an expensive mud-pack from a beautiful ceramic jar. That was about the nearest she'd come to poverty. Simply to make her way to the university by bus would be an achievement of sorts, a beginning, at least.

An hour later, Carmen Helena knew she was lost. Either the micro hadn't gone where she thought it was going, or it had passed the university and she hadn't recognised the place to get off because of the press of bodies all around her. Now the bus was in some run-down part of the city she had never seen before.

Several times she had tried asking el *cobrador*, the
conductor, a boy of about fifteen or sixteen, where they
were and if she should get off, but he was always too
busy to answer her—busy collecting money, spotting
potential passengers who were hailing their bus as one
might a taxi, shouting information to the driver about
the proximity of rival micros, helping him negotiate a
route through the traffic as swiftly as possible. The
passengers merely stared at her stupidly as if she were
a being from another planet or argued with each other
about where the micro did or did not go. Finally, in a
brief slack moment, the young cobrador told her that
she should have alighted several blocks ago. The best
thing, he said, was to step off at the corner here and—

'Bandit to the rear! Gap opening to your right!'

She was almost pushed off as the micro lunged
forward into the stream of traffic.

At a small corner cafe which sold cheap and brightly
coloured bottled drinks, but provided no glasses, Carmen Helena hesitated. She could use the cafe phone and
order a taxi. The girl behind the counter laughed.

'Telephones in this area? That's a joke!'

Anyway, telephoning would have been a rich person's
solution. Carmen Helena asked the girl about buses. The
girl shook her head. She hardly ever went to that part
of the town, the price of everything was so much
higher there. However, a man at a nearby table gave
her directions. Turn right out of the door and one block
east, on Calle Thirty-nine there were plenty of buses
going where she wanted to go.

'Gracias, señor.'

'De nada.'

As she walked eastwards Paco laughed inside her head:
'You're like the eighteenth-century French aristocracy
playing at being shepherdesses. You're just playing at it,
merely playing at it.' Carmen Helena was walking faster

and faster, down the rough lane. 'That's right Paco, have a good sneer!' She stopped to remove a stone from her shoe. The lane down which she had been directed had steadily become narrower. Washing, slung from one house to another, hung stiffly, clothes washed in cold water, drying with a film of dust on them. Then she saw the three men in the lane. They were blocking her retreat—one of them was the man who had given her directions in the cafe. Two more men appeared on the other side of her. Throwing her handbag into the middle of the lane, she backed hard against the wall. The man from the cafe nodded at her approvingly, picked up the bag and walked on. They all walked on down the lane. Then one of them glanced over his shoulder, turned and came back.

'Take your shoes off!'

Carmen Helena handed them to him.

'Now your dress!'

'No! No, please!' She crossed her arms over her breasts.

The man reached forward, prised her arms away, unzipped her dress and wrenched it downwards past her hips, till it fell to the ground. She screamed. He slapped her hard. In her bra and slip, she crouched, trembling. He picked up the dress and gave a scornful laugh.

'Waiting to be raped, are you? Well, you're out of luck! Stupid, rich cow!'

A door opened. A stout woman scuttled out, took Carmen Helena by the arm and led her into a small, smoke-filled room. She was aware of being guided into a chair. Four children between the ages of two and seven sat on a bed watching black and white television. A man, who was obviously sick, lay in another bed. The woman gave Carmen Helena a cup of black coffee from an enamel jug on a grease-encrusted stove. The children stared at her, then went on watching television.

The woman spoke to her reassuringly. Carmen Helena replied, without knowing what the words were that came out, reliving those arms reaching towards her. She closed her eyes.

'Feeling better?'

Carmen Helena opened her eyes. 'Yes, I think so. Thank you.'

This, Carmen Helena realised, was the entire living space for the whole family. A space hardly any bigger than what she thought of as 'her little cubicle' at the university. There was nothing in the room which, if it had been in her parents' house, wouldn't have been thrown out long ago: the cracked cup in her hand, the rickety beds, the clothes hanging on a piece of rope slung across the wall.

'What can I wear?'

The woman reached up and pulled down a cotton skirt, clean but stained and patched, and a faded woollen cardigan, stiff and shapeless, the life pummelled and squeezed out of it. From a battered suitcase beneath the bed she produced a pair of old worn canvas sneakers.

'Will you tell me your name and give me your address so that I can send these back to you and—and repay you for your kindness?'

The woman looked at the floor and made no reply. Carmen Helena repeated her words. The woman thrust the clothes into her arms and shook her head.

'I know you mean well, señorita, but you cannot help us. In three hours from now we are being evicted. We shall be homeless. Who knows where we shall be . . . or what will become of us?'

'Dear God, and here am I taking your clothes from you!' She buried her head in her hands. The woman bent over her.

'Are you all right, dear? Is anything wrong?'

'I am so much more all right than you—that's what is wrong.'

A weary, resigned shrug.

'Mama, will we be able to watch Robin Hood before we go?'

'Yes, my darling, yes.'

'At least tell me your name.'

'Lydia.'

'Where will you go, Lydia? You and the children and your father?'

'He's my husband. Illness has made him old.'

'But he's far too ill to move.'

Lydia gave a bitter laugh. 'Yes. He will die.'

'Isn't there anything I can do to help you? There must be something.'

The eldest child, a girl, without taking her eyes off the television set, said, 'You could give us your hair.'

'Estella, really! Don't listen to the silly girl. I'm sorry.'

'But Mama, you said I'd have to sell mine when it's longer. Hers is nice and long already.'

'Estella! Be quiet!' The girl's eyes travelled to a pair of scissors hanging from a nail. Carmen Helena rose from her chair and took them down. She put them into Lydia's hands.

'Cut my hair. Please. It's the very least I can do. I want you to do it.'

'I couldn't.'

'Please, for my sake. For your man's sake . . . for the children's sake.'

Slowly Lydia started chopping at the hair.

In this city full of taxis, it had never occurred to Carmen Helena that hailing one could be difficult; and now, suddenly, it was. She had started walking in a district where taxis were few and far between and not inclined to stop for a hairless pauper who

was obviously not the world's biggest tipper. Only
two bothered to pull in, and both drove off when she
tried to explain that she had no money but they would
be paid on arrival at the other end—a woman with no
papers and no means of identification, a likely story!
The nearest place Carmen Helena knew of where help
would be available was the Pan American Bank where
her friend Paula's father worked. If she could get there
before it closed she could borrow money from him, or
have him order a taxi for her. She might even be able
to go back to Lydia and give her something a bit more
valuable than a pile of curly black locks. She missed her
hair. Without it she felt strange, a different person.

She heard the shouting, the chanting, the loud-hailers,
but her mind was on the mugging, on the kindness of
Lydia, on Paco. Turning a corner, she found herself
in the midst of a fleeing mob. The group known as
'The Wives and Mothers of the Disappeared' had been
well organised. They carried 4,758 placards, each with a
name boldly printed on it—the name of a person known
to have been taken in for questioning and never released.

The mounted riot police were well organised too. They charged down the road, routing the demonstrators with thrusts of their long electric prods and vicious blows with their batons. Carmen Helena sprang aside, tripped and fell in the gutter. An armoured car drew up on the corner, pulling a trailer behind it. A thick rod of water from the water-cannon struck Carmen Helena in the back, knocking her down again, rolling her over and over, pounding her. She crawled out of its arc of fire to find a sub-machine gun being pointed at her. She was motioned against a wall, next to a dozen or more other people. A van skidded to a halt and the doors were thrown open. Her relief that she wasn't about to be executed on the spot was short-lived. She'd lost her identification papers along with her other things and it was an offence to be in the streets without them. Surely they couldn't treat her like this! Three hours ago this would hardly have been a problem—a sweet smile, a mention of her father's name, some crisp notes politely but discreetly changing hands. So easy. But that was three hours ago. Three hours ago she had belonged to a different world, she'd had the protection of wealth and power and privilege: now she had crossed some invisible line.

A petrol-bomb exploded nearby. The police took cover behind the van. The woman next to Carmen Helena gave her a push.

'Escape while you can! Run!'

And run she did. In her torn, drenched clothes, one shoe missing, bruised, angry, outraged, relieved, Carmen Helena arrived at the Pan American Bank. The chauffeur was holding the door of the Chevrolet open, Paula's father was climbing in. Carmen Helena rushed forward and tapped the window. Paula's father looked straight through her, wound the window even tighter shut and averted his face.

'It's me! It's Carmen Helena! Please, I— '

But the doorman was pushing her away and the Chevrolet was driving off.

In this stupid, inefficient city, she discovered you could only call collect if it was long-distance.

'Just the price of a phone call. Please, all I want is to make a phone call.'

But the passers-by ignored her.

'Please, señor, won't you help me? All I need is the price of a phone call.'

She was too old for sympathy, too well fed, no baby in her arms. It was hopeless. She sat on the kerb and cried. The Pan American Bank was closed; it was a long, long walk out to the respectable suburb where her apartment was, and even further to where her parents lived; the university was nearer, but even that seemed miles and miles when you had to walk. She had always thought of the university as being quite close to the Pan American Bank, only fifteen minutes by car at the very most; now it could be on the other side of the moon. Then Carmen Helena remembered the charity luncheon her mother was helping to organise. The Santander Hall, in the centre of town, had been booked for the occasion. That was quite near. These events, which involved paying enormous sums of money to be mentioned in the gossip columns as having been there, and to be photographed alongside other people who had also paid handsomely for their ticket, usually started at about two-thirty in the afternoon. The luncheon would be under way already.

The doorman of the Santander Hall laughed out loud when she told her story.

'Best one I've heard all week. Now push off!'

'But it's true! My mother will reward you well if you help me.'

'Listen, puta, I don't know what your game is, but I recognise a whore down on her luck when I see one. I could lose my job for less, so beat it, before I beat you.'

The luncheon was being held in a banqueting room on the first floor of the hall. Round the back was an unguarded yard and a shed. By clambering onto the roof of the shed, Carmen Helena was able to peer through a window into the banqueting room. It was barred, of course—beautiful wrought-iron work, in delicate filigree patterns which made you forget its purpose was not decorative. Inside the room about a hundred people were seated at a table, eating. She had forgotten, until that moment, that this was a fancy dress occasion with dancing afterwards.

The theme was Copetin. Copetin was a cartoon street kid who appeared in the newspaper *El Tiempo*. Comic, cheeky, tough but angelic, wise and innocent at the same time, a daily outwitter of pompous officialdom, Copetin made his well-heeled fans feel easier in their minds about the wretched children they saw in the streets; Copetin assured them that being on the streets was really an enjoyable game. For some of the guests it was an excuse to wear the fashionable gamin look, others had employed their tailors in running up little numbers from exquisite patchworks of silk. One had cleverly come as Pinocchio . . . it was Paula's father! And there was her own mother, looking so elegantly poor. Carmen Helena banged on the bars and shouted. She shouted again and kept on banging and shouting. Nobody looked up, nobody saw or heard her. Gradually, with the heat and moisture from bodies enjoying good food, good wine and good conversation, the window misted up and the people inside faded from view.

Relative Values

On the narrow parapet of a stone-walled cutting lay the Panther gang, waiting for the express train into the city.

'I think maybe I'd lose count of the days but for this train,' Angel said. If it was the day for the Great Train Robbery it was a Friday, and this would be the third train he'd robbed. They were arranged along the parapet in groups of three, each group ready to drop on to the roof of a carriage as it passed underneath. Quinque, Angel and Angelina were in one group. Quinque consulted his stolen wrist-watch. It was 4.47 in the morning.

'Another three minutes and it'll be here!'

Normally, with trains, there were no timetables, only rumours. But the express trains were run by gringos—people with strange ideas about punctuality.

So many of the Panther gang had been 'tidied away' off the streets before Independence Day that Angel and Angelina had been allowed in without having to prove their worth by fighting someone for a place or passing one of the gang's 'ordeals'. There weren't many girls in the gang, but Angelina had narrow shoulders and no breasts and could be useful when it came to squeezing down a chimney or through a small window. Once she'd grown breasts she'd have other uses, of course.

'Got all the gear, Angel?'

Angel patted his pockets and nodded. If, for some reason, they were unable to climb through a carriage window, Quinque had shown them how to use the telescopic aerials pinched off cars as fishing-rods to hook out clothes and bags and anything else that looked worthwhile.

Angel's heart pounded. In his gut and in his dreams the train had begun hurtling towards this moment hours ago. Angelina clutched his arm.

'Here it comes!'

'Get ready, you two. Same as before. You first, Angel.'

The banshee wail as it entered the far end of the tunnel; the rumbling, panting approach, louder, louder, louder. Angel eased himself towards the edge of the parapet, arms tensed, legs bunched for the spring, quivering on the point of no return. A deep breath. An explosion of noise, smoke, steam, a whirlwind of hot cinders stinging his face, singeing his hair.

'Now!' Quinque shouted. In one wild heartbeat Angel launched himself outwards, felt his feet hit the roof of a swiftly-moving carriage and pitched forward on his face. Lying on the roof of the next carriage were Angelina and Quinque. Angel crawled along the swaying roof towards them, aware that Quinque would have sauntered it, hands in pockets. Then the terrifying flop across the gap from one carriage to the other, which made Quinque double up with laughter. All three lowered themselves over the side. The carriages were the width of the train, each one self-contained with bunks, toilet and shower.

'Try this one,' Quinque whispered, nudging Angelina. 'Remember, only six minutes to jump-off point.'

Angelina squeezed through a narrow gap at the top of the window. After a brief tussle with a catch, the window slid open.

'Now you, Angel. In you go! Five minutes, five seconds. Buena suerte!'

Inside the jolting carriage, a family of three was asleep, the father in the top bunk, a little girl and the mother in the lower bunk. Angelina grabbed a silk slip and passed it to Quinque who had stayed outside. Angel was aware of his sister moving about silently, merging into the shadows, her presence only detectable by the occasional gleam of white teeth. He lifted a portable video player. No—too heavy to jump with and too conspicuous to carry through the streets. A handbag, clothes, shoes—there was usually something lying around. Nothing. He tried to open a large trunk on a stool at the foot of the bunk. It was locked.

'Four minutes!' Quinque called softly.

The mother turned in her sleep, her breath ruffling the hair on the back of the little girl's neck. Angel knelt, as if in a trance, brushing his cheek against the woman's, then straightening, he stood transfixed, overwhelmed, as the train hurtled through the dawn.

'For Christ's sake!' Quinque hissed, 'How much longer are you going to stand there? Three minutes! Take something! For Christ's sake take something!'

The flickering girders, the echoing, metallic roar as the train passed over the bridge. The carriage lurched. A framed photograph, half under the mother's pillow, slid forward. Angel caught it before it hit the floor and put it in his pocket.

Quinque's voice was urgent. 'Thirty seconds!'

The man in the top bunk was shouting, missing his footing on the step-ladder, falling. And then Angel was through the door and swinging up on to the roof. Angelina was already there, a bundle of clothes under her arm, Quinque beside her, his eyes fixed on his watch.

'Ready,' he called. 'Jump!'

Sand heaps in the builder's yard broke their fall. Angel pitched forward, did a somersault and rolled away before the next lot of bodies hit the sand. Bulldozer, the gang leader, helped Quinque to his feet.

'How did it go?'

'OK.' Quinque said. 'But Angel didn't take much. I
don't know what got into him today.'

The gang moved out of the builder's yard into a blind
alley. While one of them kept watch at the entrance to
the lane, the others displayed their loot in turn, cheering
or groaning as each item was held up for inspection,
passing comment on which receiver in La Olla might
be interested and how much he'd pay for it. A boy
received a kicking for returning with a beautiful pigskin
case—almost worthless because it was tooled in gold
letters with a name and address. Angel took the framed
photograph from his pocket. The frame seemed to be
made of some dull, tarnished metal, but the photograph
was pure gold. It could have been—no, it was—his own
mother, holding him, loving him, looking at him the
way she did in his fantasies. It was the most wonderful
thing he'd ever seen.

'Angel! What did you get?' Bulldozer demanded. He
took the frame from Angel's hand, opened the back,
removed the photograph and tore it into little pieces.
'Don't want it to be identified, do we?' He scratched
the frame, then rubbed it. 'Solid silver!' he exclaimed,
turning an approving smile upon Angel. 'Now here's
someone who knows the value of things!'

16

Fancy Wrapping

The malaria pill stuck in Warren's throat.

'Whisky on the rocks!' he ordered, catching the eye of the hotel barman. Flipping open his wallet, Warren Sheldrick extracted a greenback, his eyes sliding off the family photograph in its perspex compartment—himself, the wrong side of forty and a lot fatter then he'd like to be, Rachel, his wife, her looks beginning to fade, and Amy, their ten-year-old daughter, laughing the way she used to laugh before her kidney began to fail. Clapping his wallet shut he downed the pill in one large gulp.

'I'm with CIA,' he would announce. It made people sit up and take notice. Not the Central Intelligence Agency but Chemodrugs International Associates. He took another gulp of whisky. The very thought of venturing beyond the hotel made his mouth go dry. Out there was alien territory. The Hilton, with its carpeted lounge and its soft music and scented air, was an outpost of civilisation, of the USA. Yesterday Warren had crossed the threshold of the automatic doors. The smell! The beggars!

Although this little jaunt to South America had been dressed up as a wonderful opportunity, he knew he had been out-manoeuvred. That arsehole Nielsen had sent him to this goddamned corner of the world to get him out of the way. Nothing like removing a guy from the centre of things if you want to castrate him career-wise. You had to admit, though, Nielsen had done well to muscle in on the US Government's aid plan for health improvement in developing countries. He must remember not to call them Third World countries any more. There'd been some pretty fierce competition to beat off to get to that particular honeypot. Health aid was a cut-throat business, no doubt about it. There were strings attached, of course. Countries receiving the Health Improvement Loan could only place contracts for medical supplies and equipment with US based companies.

'Charity ends at home,' Nielsen had said. 'Foreign aid is for the health of American business, so just make sure we come out of this with rosy cheeks.'

Warren rattled the ice in his glass.

'Same again. No, make it a double this time.'

'Si, señor.'

The word 'double' reminded Warren of 'the Double I Option'. Nielsen was particularly keen that he scored a touchdown on that one.

'Image Improval, Warren. The shareholders want something that makes us out to be a caring and concerned company, something that will give them a warm glow, make them feel good about themselves, something which will tell them that, by investing in CIA, they are contributing to the well-being of the world's poor.'

Warren had responded with his usual bland smile, remembering with secret satisfaction Nielsen's prize booboo: off-loading a large consignment of unsaleable pills for obesity on an area hit by famine.

So, Nielsen was a bastard. Basically, though, Warren reassured himself, CIA was OK. He wouldn't work for a company that wasn't caring and concerned, of course he wouldn't. Some things were just normal business practice, just the way things worked. If your competitor claimed five things his product would cure, you named six; if he disclosed three adverse reactions, you'd have to be stupid if you disclosed more than two. After all, CIA was bringing drugs and medicines to people who'd never had them before. You couldn't do that unless you stayed competitive and covered your costs.

Warren glanced impatiently at his gold wrist-watch. Where on earth was the guy who was meant to be taking him to the meeting? No wonder this country was down in the minor leagues, if this was how they did business. According to the terms of the aid programme, 'goods may be repackaged by the consumer country to suit local conditions'—which was what the meeting was about, a preliminary get-together with the business barons of the city who wanted a piece of the action.

'Señor Sheldrick? Señor Warren Sheldrick?'

Warren looked up. An expensively-suited, middle-aged man introduced himself as Juan Lopez, President of the Confederation of Commercial and Business Interests. He was honoured, he said, to escort Warren to the Avispa Country Club where the meeting was to take place.

'A beautiful country,' Warren remarked from the comfort of the Lincoln Continental's deep upholstery.

'A country of the four Cs,' Juan Lopez said. 'Our four main money-makers—cocaine, coffee, copper and communism.'

'Communism is bullshit! Hogwash! You can forget all that claptrap about equality. The prizes go to the strongest. Always have and always will.'

Juan Lopez smiled and nodded his agreement.

'Nonetheless, communism is our most profitable product. We receive millions of dollars to combat its threat. We couldn't do without it. If we didn't have any communists we'd have to invent them.' Seeing Warren's doubtful expression, Juan Lopez added, 'But don't worry, democracy will survive as long as we make quite sure the wrong people don't get a chance to make their voices heard.'

The Lincoln halted at some lights. A one-armed man tried to attract Warren's attention, waving packets of Marlboro cigarettes for sale. Warren looked the other way. Two boys of about the same age as his daughter stood with supplicant hands beside his window, feral boys with scabby shaven heads and eyes which suddenly flashed green as Warren's air-conditioned bubble eased forward.

Beneath crystal chandeliers, in a room overlooking the polo field and the hangars of the privately owned small aircraft and microlites, Warren spoke to the well-fed assembly, ending with some details about 'the Double I Option'. The pharmaceutical lobby in the USA, he explained, was concerned about the bad publicity it had been receiving in connection with its activities in the Third World, that is to say, in the Developing World. Warren knew it would be tactless to go into too much detail, since many of those present were party to some of these practices, such as the omission of warnings that went with the same product in the USA, the making of exaggerated claims which would have been illegal back home, the dumping of medicines from the States whose useful life had expired. He merely told them that there was felt to be a need for image improval and there was money available to them from the US Government via CIA to do it.

'For the right proposal, there's up to a quarter of a million dollars going. I look forward to receiving your proposals, gentlemen.'

Back in his hotel Warren was wondering how to ask the porter to find him a young girl for the night when the phone rang. It was the reception desk to say that Juan Lopez was downstairs waiting for him. After the customary ten minutes of small talk Juan Lopez let it be known that he had been well briefed. He knew about Amy and her need for a new kidney, and about the frustrations of waiting for a suitable donor. As director of the Juan Lopez Foundation Clinic, he could arrange everything. The operation had been performed many times in his clinic. This was a violent city. Daily, people's lives ended abruptly with their organs in good condition. Wealthy people flew in from all over the world to exchange new organs for old, no questions asked.

'Is it all legal?' Warren wanted to know.

Juan Lopez studied the ash on the end of his expensive cigar.

'The law is like a knife, my friend: it never cuts the one who holds the handle.'

He would guarantee that if Amy came to the clinic, within a day of completing the necessary tests on her, they could perform the operation.

'And the cost?' Warren asked.

'The cost of a new life for your daughter,' Juan Lopez said, 'is a firm contract making Juan Lopez Enterprises the sole agent through which CIA's share of the Health Improvement Loan is handled.' He leant forward. 'She will be in expert hands.'

Warren's grip tightened round his whisky glass.

'I'd like to visit the clinic to check it out,' he heard himself saying. 'And I'll have to speak to my wife about it.'

But he knew already what his answer would be.

Warren's taxi passed through streets of luxury villas to houses of uncemented breeze blocks on whose flat roofs washing fluttered and hens were kept in cages.

The driver said, 'Meeting someone, señor?' Not that he cared, but his passenger was going to the airport without any luggage and he was hoping for a return fare.

'I'm meeting my wife and daughter. Amy, that's my ten-year-old daughter, is coming here for an operation.'

The driver said, 'You mean there's some branch of medicine in which we're more advanced than the mighty USA?'

Warren squirmed on the back seat.

'Well, in fact, it's because kidneys are easier to get here.'

'Ah yes, there's no end to the natural wealth of this wonderful country of ours—tin, zinc, copper, tropical timbers, kidneys, hearts, livers . . .'

At the next traffic lights a barefoot boy offered the driver a set of windscreen wipers at a very reduced price. The driver purchased them, ignoring the disapproving click of Warren's tongue.

'It wouldn't be allowed back home. No wonder there's a flourishing trade in stolen spare parts when guys like you encourage it. I want to stop at the Plaza San Martine, it's on the way to the airport, I'm told. I'll be about twenty minutes.'

The Plaza San Martine was where they were filming the mobile dispensary, the proposal for 'the Double I Option' which Warren had selected for development, not because of its merits, but because it was the one submitted by Juan Lopez. It wasn't a bad idea, though: a mobile dispensary going round the city, doling out free medical aid to the waifs and strays who lived on the streets. Big on the Bambi factor. Warren stepped out at the corner of the plaza just as the person he had arranged to meet also arrived in a taxi. She was an American journalist, a blonde Amazon sent by *Gloss* magazine and accompanied by a South American photographer. They shook hands.

Parked nearby was a van on the side of which was a board with the words, 'The CIA-Juan Lopez Enterprises

Mobile Dispensary.' A camera crew was filming a line of ragged children gratefully receiving the healing gifts of the developed world. A child was being handed two large pink capsules which he or she (Warren wasn't sure which) swallowed with the aid of a cup of orange juice proffered by a smiling helper, very definitely female, who was wearing a T-shirt with CIA prominently displayed across it.

'Cut!' shouted the director. 'How many more times have I got to tell you to look both pathetic and grateful at the same time! OK, we'll do it again.'

His assistant barked out, 'Stand by for take ten!'

The blonde Amazon's interest perceptibly sharpened.

'Am I to understand, Warren, that this is all pretence?' She moved to the van and lifted the sign. Underneath it read, 'Frederico for the best van hire in town.'

Warren started on some incoherent, stammering explanation but she cut him short with a hard-edged laugh.

'Don't worry, this will never reach the pages of *Gloss*. My bosses are well and truly in the pockets of certain political and commercial interests. I've had my orders about the kind of copy I'm to send in.'

'I know. You wouldn't be here otherwise.'

'All the same, just as a matter of personal interest—a quarter of a million dollars, Warren? A quarter of a million! Surely you could afford to do more than hire a van for a couple of weeks and play at having a dispensary.'

Warren mopped his brow and looked at the ground.

'Where did it all go, Warren?'

'Not into my pocket, I can assure you. So don't look at me as if it was my fault. It's everything about this goddamned country's fault! Hell, you can't so much as twitch an eyebrow but a dozen people expect a percentage of the action, a pay-off, a backhander.'

He sketched the scenario for her. There were senators, government officials and people in high places who had interests in rival companies who had to be 'squared'. They wanted compensation for the fact that Juan Lopez Enterprises had been chosen for the project and not one of the companies on whose boards they sat. If compensation wasn't forthcoming they would use their influence to demand inquiries and cause delays. Then there was Colonel Arcinegos, the official watchdog on anything filmed within the country—some pretty heavy 'expenses' had been needed to keep him sweet. Not to mention a host of minor officials, the local police . . .

'Hell, the number of permits it suddenly becomes necessary to obtain whenever anyone smells money is incredible! Jesus, this project has got more parasites attached to it than a dog has fleas!'

What Warren didn't mention was the huge sum he'd paid to Juan Lopez to organise, equip, stock and staff this non-existent fleet of vans. Nor did he tell her that Image Improval also included preventing Image Tarnish, in other words, paying people to keep quiet about things that would take the shine off the whole project, like the drugs CIA had 'field-tested' out here prior to their release in the States and which had turned out to have nasty side-effects.

'The feller with the stethoscope, I suppose he's not a real doctor,' the blonde Amazon said.

'Nope.'

'And the kids he's examining? You're going to tell me they're all his relatives earning a little pocket money.'

'Close enough.'

'So what do the real street kids, the ones it was meant for, what do they get out of it?'

Warren jingled the loose change in his pocket and produced a fistful of coins.

'About this much.'

'My God, it's unbelievable!'

'Yes, luckily it is. As long as we've got the film to show for it there won't be too many questions asked.'

Warren stared at the coins in his hand, then at a sweet vendor with a tray slung from his neck, who had appeared on the scene. Finally he looked at a group of urchins watching the proceedings.

He turned to the photographer.

'Those ones over there, are they, you know . . . are they genuine?'

Warren approached the group with a bag of wrapped toffees. The boys rapidly rearranged themselves, strongest at the front, weakest at the back. Hands plunged into the bag. Except for those who had grabbed the toffees from the top of the bag, they were all spitting out what they'd taken or throwing them away in disgust.

'They say you've given them stones,' the photographer explained. 'The man sold you stones wrapped in pretty papers.'

'The lousy swindler!' Warren exploded. 'Something should be done about that kind of thing!'

He sat down on the running-board of the pretend mobile dispensary. Take ten, it seemed, had been a success. He remembered that, with all the worry about Amy, he had not taken his malaria pill this morning. Not daring to risk the orange juice, he tried to work up enough saliva before popping the pill into his mouth. Again it stuck in his throat. This time the sugar coating dissolved, exposing the horrible taste beneath.

'I heard about your little girl,' the blonde Amazon said 'I got this for her. It's a pop-up picture book for while she's convalescing.'

'Thanks a million. Well, a quarter of a million, anyway,' Warren smiled wanly. Maybe it was the

strain of waiting for the operation, but there was a
tear running down his cheek. Well, she could think
him weak if she wanted; after all, he was a caring man,
wasn't he?

Appointment with Death

Nelsón and Angel loitered, studying the display in the window of a small tienda which sold Indian herbs, magical spells, snake powders, iguana lard, aerosol sprays to counteract the evil eye, packets of wood shavings to help find lost objects and cheap coloured prints of Santa Barbara. Nelsón had joined the Panther gang at the same time as Angel and his sister. Both boys were waiting for Quinque.

'Where's he got to?' Nelsón demanded, a shrill note creeping into his voice.

These days, when someone didn't show up, instead of just shrugging, you started imagining the worst. They had, as the Panthers would say, 'an appointment with Dom Roberto'—they were going to do a spot of robbing, and Quinque was the third member of their snatch team. Whether it be earrings, a necklace or a purse, the principles were the same—make sure of an escape route before starting the snatch, choose a busy place where you can disappear into the crowd, work in threes, and remember that the person making the snatch always runs towards and not away from the other two so that he can quickly slip the stolen object to one, while the other impedes the chase.

Nelsón knew very little about the other two in his team. Better not to ask. He himself never talked about his former life in the barrio any more, about the sadistic mayordomo in the mine, or his father's violent death,

about his mother, his little brothers and sisters. Quinque
swaggered up, chewing gum.

'Well, my little sparrows, ready for work?'

The three Panthers stared into a shop window in the
arcade, watching the passers-by reflected in the glass.
Nelsón selected their first mark, a woman with a basket
in which a purse nestled. She was carrying the basket
two-handed, which meant she didn't have a hand free
to grab hold of him. He nudged Quinque who nodded
agreement. While Quinque and Angel deployed themselves behind the woman, Nelsón sauntered forward,
drew level with her, made a quick snatch and darted
into the crowd, slipping the purse to Angel.

'Easy! Easy!' crowed Nelsón, dancing round the
other two when they joined up again. Returning to
the mainstream of shoppers, they followed a woman
with dangling earrings, waiting for an opportunity to
snatch them. She stepped into a taxi and the chance
was gone. Nearby, another taxi was drawn up at the
kerb. The driver lounged in the back seat with his feet
up, listening to a football commentary on the transistor
radio beside him.

'Watch this,' Angel whispered.

He knelt down and quietly peed under the car, directly
below the petrol tank.

'Señor, señor, your tank is leaking, look.'

The driver held open the door and peered out, saw
the liquid spreading into the gutter beneath his car, and
cursed. He got out to have a closer look—the radio
was in Quinque's hands and he was disappearing into
the crowd, passing it to Angel who hid it under his
loose-fitting coat.

'Let's try for a wrist-watch,' Quinque said ten minutes
later. 'This is the best time of day for it.'

In the heat of the day it was fairly common for drivers
to keep their front windows open. At traffic lights they

would sometimes stick the left elbow out to cool off, or casually rest an arm along the edge of the window. With a tug and a slash of a razor, you could have a watch off a driver in no time. Most local drivers were wise to this trick and wore their watches on the right wrist. There was always some bobo, however, waiting to be taken.

Walking slowly between two lines of halted traffic, Quinque spotted a hand drumming impatiently on the outside of the door. He sauntered past it. Slash! Off came the watch and away raced Quinque, palming it quickly to Nelsón. Quinque fell. A burley stall-owner bore down on him. Nelsón's flick-knife was in his hand, darting and weaving like the head of a snake about to strike. The man drew back, blinking. The boy was small, but the knife looked sharp. With a final flourish of his knife, Nelsón took to his heels. An armed security guard, who had been standing on duty at the entrance to the arcade, gave chase, one hand pressed to the butt of his revolver, but not yet drawing it. Of Quinque and Angel there was no sign. Nelsón raced down a side-street. No! He'd made a mistake! The street was empty, the guard might shoot. Quick!

˙ Up this one! Booted feet pounded behind him. At least two men were chasing him now. The lane ended in a cul de sac, but Nelsón knew his own territory. He knew that the four-foot wall had a ten-foot drop on the other side. He vaulted the wall, landed, rolled to his feet and was running again as the first man over the wall dropped unprepared and clutched his ankle, roaring with pain. Warned, the second man cleared the obstacle safely and tore after Nelsón, his companion screaming for revenge. Nelsón was beginning to flag, the guard to gain ground. He turned into another road, his eyes anxiously scanning the doors in the wall . . . not that one . . . not that one . . . Flinging himself to the ground, he squirmed under the bottom of the steel double-doors. The gap was too narrow for the guard, and the wall too high.

'Fat pig!' Nelsón taunted breathlessly, laughing uncontrollably.

'You'll come to a violent end, you will!' the guard bellowed. 'Your sort always do. You mark my words, a violent end!'

Nelsón capered around the junk-yard, hurling insults through the door. He was on a high higher than bazuco could ever give him. He'd downed and outwitted uniformed authority. But more than that, when he had brandished his knife, he'd seen fear in a grown man's eyes. A man like the mayordomo, like those soldiers, had been afraid of him! One day he'd have a gun. Then he'd show them he wasn't just some insignificant maggot to be trodden underfoot. He'd show the world that he mattered.

His Eminence

Muttering to himself, Paco strode along the pavement, his pace slowing or speeding up according to the heat of the argument inside his head as he rehearsed what he would say. Paco was only a minute away from the Archbishop's palace. In his pocket was the letter summoning him to the presence of His Eminence Cardinal Noberto Umana.

'Miracles! Miracles! Miracles performed here!' announced Ernesto the puppet, banging a drum. 'Roll up, roll up for The Feeding of the Five!'

Paco's pace slowed as he neared the makeshift booth of the puppet show from which a silver balloon was straining at its leash. Not wanting to be late, he had arrived far too early. He stopped to watch.

'Come and see the miracle play!' Ernesto cried. 'Oye! I've just realised. He didn't give me a part in it! Why is that, I'd like to know? After all, as the most popular, the most handsome, the most talented puppet in the company— '

A hand pulled him down and the play began. On Busca's left hand were five finger-puppets, dressed in rags.

'We are the starving multitude, we are the five thousand!'

On his right hand was one larger puppet, the white-robed figure of Christ. In a basket beside the Saviour were five fresh loaves and two fishes, such as could be bought in any of the city's market places.

'Feed us! Feed us!' moaned the five thousand, bowing to the ground when Busca clenched his fist. 'We are the poor and we are hungry!'

On hearing these words, Christ sank from view below the stage to reappear wearing a pair of rose-tinted spectacles and with a top-hat substituted for his shining halo.

'I am the first of the five. Being a government minister, of course I'd care for the poor . . . if we had any poor. But we have no poor. The poor do not officially exist—and that's official.'

And, so saying, he bent down, grabbed a loaf in both hands and swallowed it in one gulp.

'Feed us, feed us!' moaned the five thousand. The top-hat was replaced by a bishop's tall, gold-embroidered mitre and the poor were berated for wanting riches in this life when they could look forward to so much in the next. The bishop, too, devoured a whole loaf all by himself.

'Feed us! Feed us!'

People were staring at Paco as if they expected him to object, or defend the bishop, or forbid the play to continue. He studied his shoes and said nothing. Loyalty to the Church, personal loyalty to his Archbishop, loyalty to those who really needed him, loyalty to the true teachings of Christ. Engrossed in his own internal debate, he missed the third scene. Possibly it was a rich landowner justifying himself, he wasn't sure.

Now the larger puppet was a fat, cigar-smoking banker with dollar bills stuck in his hat. Holding one of the fish in both hands, he wagged it at the crowd, lecturing them about the terrible dangers of having enough, something to do with undermining the economy. A little Indian boy, who had been standing at the side of the booth, took the cigar out of the puppet's mouth and stuffed the fish between its jaws, silencing it. The crowd applauded. The fish disappeared down the puppet's throat and it started talking again. The boy repeated the performance with the other fish. With its tail protruding between his lips like a forked and silvered tongue, the rich banker exhorted his public to throw away or destroy their surplus stock, then abused them for their selfishness, for their lack of consideration for delicate price structures and sensitive market forces.

'Feed us! Feed us!' came the response.

The fifth pillar of society sprang up wearing the uniform of the country's protectors, la policia. He beat the starving ones over the head with his baton.

'Ignorant fools! Surely you can see that the more of you there are the more money we must spend on maintaining security, preventing crime and repressing riots. Of course there's none left for scum like you!'

And he gobbled up a loaf. At the bottom of the basket lay the last loaf, fashioned like a sub-machine gun. He lifted it out and shot the five thousand.

'Well, there you are then! It's much easier to get rid of the poor than to get rid of poverty! The perfect solution!'

As the bare-headed Christ stooped to retrieve his halo, it seemed to Paco that the eyes looked straight into his own. A clock struck the quarter-hour.

'My appointment! I'm late!'

Paco ran up the broad steps of the Archbishop's palace and rang the bell.

He was shown into a book-lined study furnished with deep, leather armchairs, framed photographs and carpets of Aztec design. He noted with a wry smile that on a chessboard inlaid with jade and onyx, a red queen of exactly the same hue as the robes the Archbishop would be wearing was poised to take a pawn. He paced the room, passing a glass-fronted cabinet which

housed a silver communion cup of ancient design.
Stopping beneath a silver Christ on a silver cross,
Paco crossed himself. 'What would you do, Lord, if
you were in South America today? Forgive me, Lord,
how could I forget? You are here, you do suffer with
the poor.'

Why didn't His Eminence Cardinal Noberto Umana come? Was it a demonstration that he had the power to keep inferiors waiting? Was the Archbishop busy with more important matters? Or was he giving him time for humility and reflection?

Through the window at one end of the room leaked sounds of the outside world, the hammering and banging of some kind of construction work, a football match getting under way in the stadium. And Ernesto shouting.

'Roll up, roll up for The Feeding of the Five! Second sitting starting soon!'

The puppet show was in the street below. Paco leaned out of the window. The silver balloon, with its sad and its funny face, was floating level with the window so that he could almost touch it.

'Roll up folks! I particularly recommend the policeman in this show, you'll enjoy the policeman, an iron fist in a velvet glove, you might say. I know you'll be disappointed I don't have a part, but— '

'Father Francisco?'

Paco swung round. 'Your Eminence!'

Yes, a red queen, or perhaps a frog, a white-haired frog about to open its wide mouth, flick out a long tongue and devour a fly. Cardinal Umana extended his hand. Paco kissed his ring.

Cardinal Umana said, 'You've come to the palace on a noisy day, I'm afraid. A football match this side, work on the cathedral on the other, and goodness knows what's going on down in the street.'

'Nothing major wrong with the cathedral, I hope, Your Eminence.'

'It's built on unsure foundations, so it seems. Underneath it are the tunnels of a disused silver mine and they're starting to collapse.' The Archbishop lifted the silver communion cup from the display cabinet. 'As a

matter of fact, this was made from what they got out
of that mine.'

There was a roar from the football stadium. Paco said,
'We lost last week. Who's playing today?'

'Junior League, cup-tie,' the Cardinal said. 'From here
it always sounds as though abusing the referee is a major
part of the entertainment.'

'Perhaps, Your Eminence, it's the only place they
can raise their voices against authority without being
arrested.'

'That, Father Francisco, is precisely what I wanted
to warn you about. You, too, have been raising your
voice against authority. You have been making speeches
without my permission and challenging things that you,
a priest, have no business to challenge. In short, your
dabbling in politics must stop.'

'But how can we love our neighbour and not struggle
against the injustice which dehumanises him? And since
this injustice stems from— '

'I should not have to remind you, Father Francisco,
that the Church has only one husband, who is Christ.
It cannot be married to any political creed or system.'

'Can it be wrong to want to help the poor and the
oppressed?'

'When the gospels refer to the poor, they mean the
spiritually poor. It is not for the Church, nor for any
of its priests, to pick out one social group. The Church
belongs to all groups equally.'

In the football stadium the crowd roared and roared
again, reaching a crescendo of excitement. Cardinal
Umana walked to the window. He frowned at the
bobbing silver balloon.

'If ever a leader emerges who can inspire that kind
of passion and commitment from the poor, what
a bloodbath there will be!' He closed the French

windows and shivered. 'As for playing with those street sparrows . . . you are not, despite your name, a second St Francis.' The Cardinal held up his hand, silencing Paco's protest. 'No, they are outside legitimate society. I would much prefer to see you supporting respectable causes like the League of Alcoholics Anonymous, or working in our schools or sports programmes to preserve our young Catholic men from vice, rather than stimulating the animal instincts of the rabble and inciting men to sins of envy and covetousness.'

'Feed us! Feed us!' moaned the five thousand.

Cardinal Umana put an arm on Paco's shoulder and steered him to a row of framed photographs on a shelf.

'I understand your feelings, Francisco. Paco. Look at these photographs: that's me as a missionary in the jungles of Peru. And this is me working with the rural poor. Yes, zeal is natural in the young. But so is pride. The pride which leads you into thinking you know better than those appointed by God to guide and direct you.'

'Feed us! Feed us!' moaned the five thousand.

'I want your assurance,' Umana continued, 'that there will be no more speeches, no more tracts, no more dabblings with fallen angels of whom, may I remind you, Satan is the chief.'

Paco shook his head.

'I cannot give such an assurance.'

'Then I must tell you that you are setting yourself against the very clear norms of ecclesiastical discipline and law. Furthermore you are in danger of separating yourself from the teachings of the Church.'

They both paced the room. The hammering and thumping of the shoring-up work began again.

'The first duty of the Church is survival,' Noberto

Umana said as their paths crossed. Past the red jade
queen, past the silver communion cup in the glass-
fronted cabinet, round the globe in its carved stand.
'You would do well to consider, Father Francisco, what
the consequences would be were the Church to set itself
against those in power.'

The Cardinal stopped his pacing and stood in front of
Paco, 'Francisco, you're a good man, but I fear you may
also be a foolish one. You have started on a path that
will lead to violence. Violence has never done anything
but destroy. I reject all forms of violence, and I will
reject those whose words or actions encourage it in any
way. Will you not change your mind and give me the
assurance I seek?'

'I cannot do that.'

'In that case I give you your final warning. Any
actions by you which do not have my prior approval
will result in disciplinary procedures being set in motion.
And that could even include reduction to the lay state. Is
that clear?'

'Oh yes, you make yourself very clear, Your Eminence!' Paco was shouting now. 'The rushing stream
people call violent, the banks that press in on either
side—why does no one call these violent? Is not poverty a form of violence perpetrated by the ruling few
against the majority? Is not the death of six children
out of ten, when it could be prevented by a government that really cared, is that not a slaughter of the
innocents?'

'Feed us! Feed us!'

Cardinal Noberto Umana drew himself up to his full
height.

'Enough! You overreach yourself. I shall pray for
you.' He extended his hand. Paco knelt and kissed the
ring. The interview was at an end.

They Can't Take This Away

At ten past four on a cold Thursday morning, Busca was dragged from his sleeping place in the service elevator of El Lujomercado, down the steps and into the back of an unregistered black sedan. His abductors took with them all his puppets. This much was seen by Chinche who had been curled up on the elevator's roof. They left behind Busca's silver balloon, the one with the laughing face and the crying face. Everywhere Chinche went the balloon accompanied him, tied to the little finger of his left hand.

Begging proved, as Busca and Ernesto had said it would, a good stand-by for Chinche in the ensuing days. Sometimes people recognised Busca's balloon and gave extra; at other times, hunger was never far away, particularly on the two occasions he was robbed of his takings—once by bigger boys, once by the police. Almost as severe a hardship for Chinche was that he could no longer afford to indulge his passion for westerns. But when Chinche found a lucky charm in the gutter, a small silver-plated top-hat, he knew his luck would change.

His good fortune arrived in two separate ways. One of the TV channels had a week of Charlie Chaplin films. For a few days cheeky little tramps were popular and people gave generously. Chinche wondered about the real Charlie Chaplin and what it would be like to be famous, to have your picture in the papers and your face on the screen. Then the stabbing of a prominent citizen by a gang of kids hit the headlines and child beggars were out of favour.

The second slice of good luck came in the form of a middle-aged woman who was sweeping out a coach parked in a side-street. Her husband was the driver, she said. She was cleaning out in readiness for the 'City by Night' tour for gringo tourists, which took in the floodlit Plaza de Bolívar, the viewpoint over the city's twinkling lights, a slow crawl, with doors and windows firmly shut, through the Thieves' Market. The woman was kind and motherly. Chinche wanted to hold her hand, he wanted to put his head against her soft body, he wanted to be hugged and held tight by her. Instead, he jumped into the driving seat, wrestling with the wheel, snarling and growling like a diesel engine.

'Can you sing?' the woman asked.

Chinche negotiated a sharp bend, changing gear noisily and nodding at the same time.

'Sing something, then,' the woman said, placing her husband's peaked hat on Chinche's head, covering his eyes and ears. Chinche turned in the seat. The inside of the hat smelt of sweat and haircream.

> *I'd rather be a sparrow than a snail,*
> *Yes I would, if I could, I surely would.*
> *I'd rather be a hammer than a nail,*
> *Yes I would, if only I could, I surely would.*
> *I'd rather be . . .*

The woman clapped her hands and smiled. 'Bueno! Bueno! Yes, you'll do nicely.'

She explained that, at a prearranged point, the bus took on board an endearing little street orphan who enchanted the tourists by singing for his supper. The boy, in fact, was her own son. Unfortunately he was sick.

'You can keep ten per cent of the takings,' she said.

'Seventy per cent.'

'You're a sharp little bugger. Twenty per cent.' She didn't seem quite so motherly now.

'But it's me that's doing all the work! Fifty per cent.'

She poked Chinche with the end of her broom.

'And it's me that's got the bus and the captive audience and I can easily find someone else. Thirty per cent and that's my final offer.'

'It's a deal!'

The woman briefed him on what to do.

'Corner of Twelfth and Sixty-fifth Street, quarter after eight. And for God's sake smile.'

'I can't sing well on an empty stomach, señora,' Chinche said, with a practised whine in his voice. 'I haven't eaten for three days.'

'A likely tale!' she said, sweeping him out of the bus with her broom.

Chinche's impish smile, his grubby but cocksure manner was everything the tourists wanted in an urchin. They applauded and laughed and filled the cap with silver and asked him to repeat 'This is my lovely day' which he rendered, with a few inventions of his own when he wasn't sure of the words, in his breathy treble accompanied by expansive gestures.

> *This is my lovely day;*
> *This is the day I will remember the day I'm dying.*
> *They can't take this away;*
> *It will be always mine,*
> *The sun and the wine*
> *And wild birds crying.*
> *All happiness must fade . . .*

With his thirty per cent Chinche bought his favourite churingo sausages. He ate them thinking of Busca. It had been good while it lasted . . . Busca as well as the churingos. But nothing did last, especially if adults were involved. The rest of the money he spent on a water-pistol with a plastic holster and belt glittering with rhinestones. The meal gave Chinche energy. He dodged in and out of a traffic jam, leaping from one bonnet to another, sliding on the smooth metal. As the traffic began to move he crouched on the back fender of a Lada, keeping his head low so that the driver wouldn't see him in his mirror, imagining it was a stagecoach pursued by Indians.

'Blam! Blam!' Two Indians bit the dust.

Reaching round, he unscrewed the Lada's petrol cap and, putting his mouth to the opening, inhaled deeply. Once, twice . . . A huge beast loomed over him, roaring and snarling, its eyes flashing.

'Keep away from me! Keep away!'

The buildings on either side of the street were leaning inwards, toppling forward, about to fall on him.

'Help! Socorro!'

The traffic stopped again. Chinche toppled off the Lada and crawled between the panting vehicles to the sidewalk—where he found himself kneeling at the feet of his hero, John Wayne. Outside El Cinema Azteca Chinche stood proudly beside the poster. He was walking tall with Big John, his spurs clinking at his heels, receiving the cringing adoration of the simple but cowardly peasants. He was still in a dream state. Advancing upon him down the street, hand poised for the draw, was the baddy. With lightning speed Chinche went for his gun. A bullet thumped into Chinche's chest, hurling him backwards. He died in the street, his eyes open, still believing he was six foot tall.

The young riot policeman sounded aggrieved.

'How was I to know it was a toy gun?'

But nobody seemed particulary interested in him or his explanation. They stared at the body. One less of the pests that were beginning to creep back on to the streets after the round-up, like bugs after a fumigation. Because of Chinche's sudden and violent death, the street kids who had come running to see what was up believed that the life-force remained in his blood. They smeared blood from his wound on their faces and necks. His clothes would bring them luck in their robbing, so they removed his socks and cut pieces from his jacket.

Presently a priest pushed his way through the crowd. Some recognised him as Paco who addressed public rallies and championed the cause of the labour unions. Paco knelt and gently closed the dead boy's eyes. On the little finger of Chinche's left hand the silver balloon tugged and strained to be free. Paco released it, watching it dance in the sky, turning its two faces to the crowd below, the comic and the tragic. Then Paco went into a small shop and emerged with a wooden baker's tray. Two street children helped Paco lift Chinche onto it. Someone placed a bunch of pink carnations beside him. Paco stood over the body, head bowed. The gathering crowd shushed itself into something resembling silence. Raising his head, Paco said, 'I protest'. He didn't shout, yet he was clearly heard.

'I protest at the death of this child. The whole world should protest. Friends, I ask you to join me in the funeral procession of this boy.'

He tore down the poster of John Wayne and tenderly placed it over Chinche's shattered chest. A half-starved boy touched Chinche's silver-plated lucky charm with his own lucky dried snake's tail; another momentarily slipped his signed photograph of Maradona the football star between Chinche's fingers. Paco and six of the bigger street kids lifted the tray. Slowly they marched down the main street. People detached themselves from the crowd to join the procession; people came out of shops, out of houses; homeless boys and girls, not very different from Chinche himself, appeared from the shadows and joined the marching line. One hundred, two hundred people were marching behind the bier.

The march slowed as another procession advanced down a converging road and swung across its path—a military band, clattering cavalry, open-top cars in which bronzed and beautiful people stood, acknowledging the cheers of the crowd which lined the route.

'It's a visiting statesman of some kind,' someone said. 'There's an official reception for him today.'

Somehow Chinche's procession inserted itself amongst the pomp and glitter surrounding the statesman. Mounted soldiers in plumed helmets and full ceremonial dress flanked the humble wooden tray on which the child was carried. Then the official parade turned left, while Paco led the funeral procession to the right, up the hill towards the cemetery known as The Park of Heavenly Peace.

'Pepe, that's the private cemetery for rich people, isn't it? Why is he taking us there?'

'Well, you can be sure there's no room in the municipal graveyard. They say that on Judgement Day the graves shall open. In that case, every day of the week is Judgement Day for the likes of him and the likes of us, because the graves are emptied daily to make room for the newly dead.'

'You're right, Pepe. We're even evicted from our graves!'

The procession halted at the gates to the Park of Heavenly Peace. Paco slid open the bolts and led them past the neat, well-tended plots and sepulchres before stopping at a vast and ornate tomb. He motioned people to gather round.

'This is the family tomb of Enrique Morales, our Presidente. He calls himself the father of this country, so let one of his children be buried in his tomb. Morales cared nothing for this boy while he was alive; let him at least care for him in his death.'

Twenty men lifted and slid the heavy stone lid a few feet to one side. Several members of the press had attached themselves to the procession. A camera flashed. Paco read out the burial service from the prayer book he carried in his pocket, the circle of mourners making ragged response. The tray with Chinche's body on it was lowered into the tomb. The press cameras flashed and whirred. Tomorrow Chinche would be famous.

The Knock on the Door

Carmen Helena couldn't sleep. Lying in her satin-canopied bed she counted the strokes of the big clock in the Plaza de Bolívar. One. Two. Three. She switched on the bedside lamp. The card Paco had sent her, that was what was keeping her awake—a reproduction of the famous painting, 'The Light of the World', Christ with a lamp in his hand knocking on a door. In the past month or two some pretty loud and insistent thoughts about her lifestyle, about herself, about those less fortunate than herself had been knocking, knocking. She remembered what Paco had said to her one day at El Sagrado, his sanctuary for street children.

'Take one home in your heart,' he had said. 'And when you are safe in bed ask yourself where that child will be.'

She lay, wondering about the little boy and girl, brother and sister, she had met.

The Panthers had scattered when the other gang had attacked them. Angel and Angelina had been chased for miles. And now here they were, at three o'clock in the morning, lurking in unfamiliar streets. Outside an old Spanish-style church Angelina said, 'We'd be safe in there. They wouldn't dare hurt us in there . . . not in a church.'

Angel couldn't reach the iron ring in the heavy, metal-studded door. He made a stirrup with his hands.

'You open it, Angelina.'

She wrestled with the ring.

'It . . . it won't turn, Angel. It's either too stiff or it's locked.'

'Try knocking.'

'What's the point? There's nobody there.'

'Try anyway.'

Angelina hammered iron against iron. Nobody came. Again she hammered. She stepped down, her arms flapping, her whole body tense. A police car's claxon howled in a parallel street.

'Angel, Gatita's frightened. Gatita wants to go home.'

'No! Never!'

'What shall we do?'

'We'll curl up against the door here.'

'But supposing they find us?'

'They've probably given up looking. We'll just have to risk it.'

Angel thought about the times he'd been locked out of the shack in the barrio while César had sex with his mother. And sometimes his mother would push them both out when César was drunk. Many a time Angel had stood outside, hammering on the door, listening to her cries as César beat her. And he thought about the long, long evenings alone with Angelina and the Happydays dolls. He didn't know which was worse, being locked in or being locked out. No, he'd never go back.

Paco was working late at his desk, preparing his address to the Justice and Peace Group at the university. He heard the clock strike three. 'Hunger,' he wrote, 'is not a shortage of food, it is a shortage of justice.'

There was a knock on the door. Paco moved across the room. Was it about to happen? The arrest, or the bullet through the head? People had disappeared for saying a lot less than he had. It was the fact that he was in the public eye that protected him: he was too well known simply to disappear. There would be an outcry, riots, comments in the foreign press. But you could never be sure. Three days ago, Emiliano, his helper at El Sagrado, had been arrested.

Paco crossed himself and opened the door. A small package lay on the ground, wrapped in brown paper. A booby trap of some sort? He picked it up, slowly turned it over in his hand, then impatiently opened it. A picture. A picture of a priest, painted on corrugated glass. One hand was raised in blessing, the other arm supported a cross in the crook of the elbow. The rectangle of ribbed glass tilted in Paco's hand and the picture changed. Now he was looking at a guerrilla, fist raised in the revolutionary salute, automatic rifle across his body. Paco waggled the glass—priest, guerrilla, priest, guerrilla. Yet another communication from the FLN, the banned revolutionary party. Twice a voice had spoken to him at the confessional, and, once at El Sagrado, he'd found a screwed up piece of paper in his pocket. The message had read:

> Paco, you are too good a man to waste your talents treating the symptoms and not the cause. Revolution is the only way. Your Church has failed the people. The time has come to go another way—our way. Moses led his people out of oppression. Revolution is an exodus to a promised land.'

Martyrdom was a subtle temptation. What steps had he taken to protect himself? None. If he had the choice between a dramatic death or continuing the struggle out of the limelight, which would he choose? Death itself he did not fear. The moment of it, yes—the bullet, the knife entering his body. And he feared making the wrong choice, or making the right choice for the wrong reason. He would be guided, not by his Archbishop, but by someone else, someone, who had been regarded as subversive and had been persecuted by the religious and political establishment of his day. Nothing was clear cut, though. Was it really true to say that the country was divided into the oppressors and the oppressed? Like some kind of cancer oppression seemed to permeate all levels of society. Paco looked up at Christ on the cross.

'Lord, when I ask myself, "Who is the enemy?" I find I don't know the answer, because sometimes he appears to be all of us.'

Most of his life Paco had mistrusted those who knew exactly what the right answers were. If they saw only one clear path in front of them it was because they were narrow-minded, not because they were right. There was wisdom in having doubts. But now he prayed for certainty and the strength which certainty would give him.

Emiliano crouched in the small, windowless cell in the notorious prison known as *La Libertad*. His cell measured 1.5 m wide, 2.5 m long and 2.5 m high. A concrete ledge served as a bed. There was no furniture. An electric light bulb in the ceiling produced a harsh glare which accentuated the yellowness of the walls. An incessant noise from a generator or pump thudded overhead. In the steel door was a small Judas-hole to allow the guard to spy on the prisoner.

It would be Colonel Mendes who had ordered his arrest, a man drowning in a whirlpool of his own making. A man who had discovered that once you degrade someone it becomes imperative to degrade him even further to justify what you have done to him. Already there had been two attempts to take the colonel's life, each resulting in mass arrests and torture, each feeding the colonel's hatred for all enemies of the state and redoubling the determination of these enemies to assassinate him. Emiliano was shivering. He curled up on the concrete bunk, too terrified to want to think about what was going to happen to him, too terrified to think of anything else.

In the next cell a man screamed and screamed again and went on screaming, stopping only to give deep, harsh sobs which accelerated into more screaming. Emiliano wondered if he would be next. An hour passed, an hour during which the screaming intensified till he tore at the concrete with his nails, every nerve screwing tighter and tighter, an hour in which he arrived at the ice cold certainty that he would never leave this prison alive; an hour in which each approach of booted feet along the stone corridor made his mouth go dry, his heart palpitate.

La Libertad was a place of eternal light. Its bulbs burned night and day, twenty-four hours, turning weeks into one long, hellish day. Emiliano lost track of time. They had tortured him for quite a while. Pain invaded every part of his body. They wanted him to say that Paco was involved with the guerrillas, that he used El Sagrado to recruit young members for the FLN. Emiliano knew he only had to knock on the door of his cell and a guard would take him to where a prepared statement awaited his signature. And then there would be no more pain. The sound of a man shouting penetrated the cell. Not the hectoring shout of the interrogator, but a prisoner's shout. Emiliano had been in La Libertad long enough to tell exactly what stage the questioning had reached. The prisoner who has had a couple of blows of the fist and a belt of the baton behind the ear has a certain way of speaking, of shouting, of saying he's innocent. After he's been left two hours strung up by the thumbs he has another kind of voice. After the bath, headfirst in shit, still another. When he sounds like he's going to die any minute, you know he's had the electricity.

'I probably sounded like that,' Emiliano thought. 'Except, when it's yourself screaming, you don't hear it, not hear it—you feel the scream tearing through your muscles, the pain exploding inside you, your whole body clenching.'

How do you endure? To watch the ant crossing the cell floor, to contemplate the spider and admire the beauty of its web, these are ways of resisting. But if you can't, if worse than the electric prod, something grips your throat, allow yourself to cry. And draw comfort from the names on the wall, for someone has travelled the same long dark tunnel and found light at the end. Emiliano picked up the spoon in the plastic bowl. On the wall he scratched a poem:

> Ask not my name
> Nor if you ever knew me;
> The dreams that I've had
> Will grow without me.
> Ask not my age.
> Though dead, my body
> Will be the age
> Of every child I've freed.

The screaming had started again. For his ordeal to end, all he had to do was knock on the door.

A Perfect Day

Rounded islands of garbage peeped above the mist-filled valleys; colour was seeping into the fluttering litterscape of garish, man-made colours; mingling with the early morning mist was the acrid smell of burning rubbish. Nelsón floundered up the slope on the municipal garbage dump, through rotting vegetable matter, cinders, soggy, disintegrating paper and unidentifiable slime. He plunged and lurched through the stinking mess, encountering submerged shards of glass, rusty bedsprings and jagged cans which lacerated shins and ankles. In the good old days before the riots, the round-ups and the death-squads, the Panthers had worked the dump only once a week, on Tuesdays, the day the trucks came in from the richest areas in the east. Now, as making a living on the street became ever harder and more dangerous, they were spending more and more time on the dump.

One bag for paper, one for glass, one for metal, another for plastic bags, and one for anything else that might be saleable—five bags in all, dangling round Nelsón's waist. He was working a slope in line with Quinque, Rocco, the deaf and dumb kid born on the dump, with the strange, silent little girl, Angelina, and with Bulldozer, the leader of the Panthers. The rest of the gang were working a different section, except for their look-out, Angel, who was on one of the higher mounds. The trouble was, you never knew when the trucks were coming. Unless you got there ahead of everyone else, ahead of the old men, the junkies, the winos, the packs of wild dogs and the vultures, there was nothing left. Last week a mattress had come into the dump and they'd lost the chance of grabbing it.

Nelsón slipped and fell. He cursed the indestructibility of polythene. Everywhere lay shreds of it, torn bags of it, sheets of it, all lubricated by mud, excrement and the nameless decomposing things which a city exudes. Up a step, slide back two; try a different place, slip and slide. There were spots where the garbage was too hot to touch. Sometimes fires smouldered underground for days, even weeks, before flaring up at the surface. On occasions it was the garbage pickers themselves who lit them because glass was easier to find if the other rubbish had been burned away. Glass was fetching ten pesos a kilo at the moment.

Nelsón had soon realised that before the garbage ever reached the dump it had been well picked over. Almost every bin in the city, every public litter receptacle, and the back yard of every hotel and factory was within the territory of one gang or another, who claimed first rights on the garbage. What arrived at the dump was already twice rejected, the garbage of the garbage.

'Truck ho!' piped Angel's voice.

Slipping, falling, they ran on legs leaden from lack of food. The spongy garbage seemed to absorb Nelsón's energy, as in one of those dreams when you're running for your life and getting nowhere.

'Hurry! Hurry!' Bulldozer panted. He, too was slowing down. They topped the rise. Below, two trucks were in the act of tipping their loads. Already the vultures were there, and the dogs: walking rib-cages, with no hair, like plucked, half-rotten chickens. And a wino had beaten them to it. He was clothed in pieces of sacking and polythene tied about his person with string. He wore heavy, nailed boots. Nelsón feared those boots. They could break shins and crush feet.

The wino had found something—there was no mistaking the tell-tale swoop. He straightened, holding a sack into which he furtively peered. From the speed with which he closed it, Nelsón knew he had something worth hiding. Nelsón descended the slope in a series of huge bounds, sprinted up behind the wino and snatched the sack from his grip. More winos appeared. One blocked his path. He dodged. Two more tried to cut him off. They were cursing and aiming drunken blows at him. Vultures flapped and squawked out of the way and exploded into the air. Nelsón heaved the sack to Quinque who swung it high in the air for Bulldozer to catch and convey a safe distance up the slope. The winos lost interest in the sack and returned to plundering the treasures spilled by the departed trucks. The vultures returned. Boys, men, vultures, dogs—slowly their frenzy died away until they were no more than poking listlessly at what remained of the tippings.

A helicopter flew overhead. Two objects fell from the sky and landed on the dump about a hundred metres away.

'What are you waiting for? Run, run! Before anyone else gets there!'

Breathing hard, they looked down on two bodies, a man and a woman, disfigured by torture, but with clothes on their bodies and shoes on their feet, and the man had a gold filling in a tooth and the woman had a good head of hair.

'What a lucky day for us! What a windfall!'

Wumf! The flames responded avidly to a cupful of petrol. It was the hour of day for *El Fogota*, the gathering round the evening fire.

'El catequismo!' Bulldozer announced. 'What is the first rule by which we survive?'

'We survive by obedience to the leader!' chanted the ragged circle.

'What kind of obedience?'

'Absolute obedience!'

Wumf! Again the fire flared up, lighting gaunt faces.

'What is the second rule by which we survive?'

'To share everything with our compañeros.'

'Everything?'

'Yes, everything!'

Wumf!

'The third rule?'

'Never, never inform on a compañero.'

Wumf!

'The fourth?'

'Defend our territory at all times against rival gangs.'

They joined hands slowly circling the fire, chanting: 'Panthers rule the city!' Three times round. 'Panthers rule the city!'

Nelsón was the hero of the hour. The sack he'd grabbed had contained a full litter of puppies, a real delicacy when roasted in the ashes of the fire.

'It could pass for roast duck in the best restaurants in the city,' Quinque exclaimed, gnawing on a bone.

'It probably does,' Angel replied, taking a swig of the 'electric soup', a concoction of wood alcohol, boot polish and fermented potato peel which they had bought from the winos. Rocco bolted his food like an animal, snuffling and snarling, hardly using his fingers at all.

Quinque said, 'When I was six they stuck me in an institution. Shelter Five they called it. There were kids there who used to eat like that.' He began sorting a pile of plastic bags into different sizes. 'We were shackled to our beds and left lying in our own shit, day after day, with nothing to do but stare at the ceiling.' A doll's head, which had been tossed into the fire, changed shape as it melted, then burst into green flames. 'I'll tell you this for free, if you're ever tempted to think you've hit hard times . . . well, there's a long way to fall yet, a long way.'

Nelsón liked the idea that, comparatively speaking, he wasn't doing so badly. It gave him a kind of lift. And, now that he was no longer afraid to use a knife . . . well, it was only a matter of time before he was in the big league.

After the meal they sat around the glowing embers, bragging and swapping jokes and stories.

'I've heard tell that this dump takes more magazines and newspapers than the National Library,' Nelsón said.

'And I've heard tell,' said Bulldozer, 'how much gringos throw away. It must be great to live on a New York dump, what a life!' They marvelled and fantasised about an impossible dream. 'You could become so rich you could drive to the dump everyday in a Cadillac!'

They sat staring into the fire, silent now, busy with their own thoughts. Somewhere in the darkness a pack of stray dogs howled. The fire had been one of the best they'd ever had thanks to the coffins which the grave diggers had thrown out of the adjacent People's Cemetery to make room for the newly dead. Granted the coffins were mostly small ones, but it was good firewood all the same and they'd got a fantastic blaze going at El Fogota.

Nelsón smiled happily to himself, basking in his popularity over the puppies. He felt good about himself. And now bodies were falling from the sky again. Nelsón could hear the helicopters overhead. Tomorrow, when it was light, there'd be some great pickings to be had. In the far corner of the dump, where the silos and the furnaces were, they had started burning thousands of

tons of coffee. When their own fire died down and
the night air became too cold to stay where he was,
he could curl up with his back to the warm bricks.
Best of all—their regular pusher had shown Nelsón
how to use a needle to inject the stuff straight into his
veins instead of sniffing it. It cost a little more, but it
was much better. Brilliant, in fact. Daytimes weren't
too bad, you could hold at bay the fears, you could
swagger and make a noise, but at night . . . That was
when the fears scurried out, when the long-tentacled
memories reached out for you, when all the wrongs
and unfair things hurt the most. Night was when you
really needed something.

Nelsón's thoughts drifted pleasantly along, born upon
waves of sound from the nearby football stadium. It
was obviously a sizeable gathering, as many as there
would be for a football match or a pop concert. People
were screaming, but not out of adulation for a star;
people were groaning, but not like when their team
has missed a goal; and there were bangs which were not
like fireworks. All these things Nelsón noted through
a mind riding the magic carpet sent by La Blanca, the
Snow Queen. He floated in time to an orchestra of
rustling and shifting garbage, which whispered secret
harmonies. Crumpled sheets of plastic, reflecting the
dying embers of the fire, gleamed like the snow-clad
peaks of the Andes at sunset, glimmering in time to
the machine-gun fire from the stadium. Everything was
so beautiful, all was right with the world. It had been a
perfect day.

On Angels' Wings

Paco squeezed between the shiny hoardings, bright with promises and entered the garbage dump. He stumbled along a garbage valley, looking for . . . what had his Archbishop referred to them as? Oh yes, 'fallen angels'. The Archbishop. Another surge of black despair engulfed Paco—the Archbishop's failure to support him in his crusade for social justice; the massacre in the stadium; Emiliano arrested and no news of him; the threatening phone calls he himself had received; people he thought he knew well suddenly wary about donating funds to El Sagrado—it was all such an uphill struggle. And what had he achieved?

'There are times, Lord, when I feel like a man trying to empty the Atlantic and only a teaspoon to do it with,' he had confessed in his prayers.

Topping a rise, Paco surveyed the dump. It occupied low swamp-land unsuited to even the cheapest brick housing. To the north, on steeply rising ground, clung a shanty town, a barrio of illegal squatters. To the south-west, where the ground was more level, the land was occupied by legal tenants whose stone edifices were separated by neat lawns and paths. A private cemetery. Below this, where the plateau sloped down to the perimeter of the dump, on rockier ground, was a smaller cemetery, the People's Cemetery, which accommodated five or six times as many dead as its rich neighbour. Bordering the private cemetery, on the southern side, was the zoo. Here too the inmates were better housed than the squatters in their hovels of cardboard and flattened tin. Between the zoo and the storage silos was a high brick wall which Paco knew to be the back of the football stadium, the place where the massacre of suspected FLN members had taken place. Soldiers on ladders were preparing to whitewash over a slogan sprayed on the wall. 'Ernesto Lives' the slogan proclaimed. The football match in the stadium was in its last quarter, the crowd in full throat, twenty-thousand fans cheering like a single many-headed monster. A crescendo of excitement, a moan of despair like the cold wind from the mountains.

At the back of the football stadium, where the animal smell from the zoo mixed with the stench of the dump, was a sunless corner daubed with crude graffiti. Here, after a match, men gathered, seeking outlets for their frustrations when their team had lost. And the Panthers knew how to cater for that need. From a distance Paco could see the men on one side of the wire mesh fence, the gang members, most of whom were known to him, on the other side.

Rocco was naked and on all-fours, managing to force a barking noise from his diaphragm. Bulldozer, too, was naked and barking. They circled each other, Bulldozer sniffing at Rocco's rear. The men were laughing. Urged on by them, Bulldozer mounted Rocco and penetrated him. He was deliberately rough. Rocco squirmed and squealed and tried to bite Bulldozer's arm. A shower of coins flopped on to the garbage to be quickly picked up by the gang. In the grounds of the zoo, next to a notice which said, 'Do not harm the animals, they are your friends', were more spectators. They stood with their backs to the cages, ignoring the near-human antics of the apes. Paco sweated and cursed as he tried to make haste through the treacherous garbage.

'And now!' shouted Bulldozer, as he pulled on his

trousers, 'The moment you have been waiting for!' He raised Rocco's arm. 'This garbage-picking child, suckled by stray dogs, reared as one of the pack, speaking no language known to man, will perform an amazing feat.'

Paco broke into a run, slipping, sliding, falling. Two boys poured kerosene in a circle and set it alight. Into the circle were released rats from a sack.

'Jungle-child will kill fifty rats inside five minutes . . . with his hands tied behind his back!'

Rocco entered the arena.

'Now!' shouted Bulldozer.

Rocco dropped to his knees. With a lightning movement of his head he bit through the back of a rat's neck. A rat fastened itself to his cheek. He ignored it, killing again and again, his jaws crunching relentlessly on neck or backbone.

'Forty! Forty-one! Forty-two!'

'Kill! Kill!' urged the crowd.

'Forty-nine . . . fifty!' Rocco stood up, his face a mass of deep incisions and loose folds of hanging flesh.

'More! More!' screamed the crowd, raining coins upon the bodies strewn around the circle.

'Kill! Kill! Ki . . .'

The shouting died away. Standing in the smoking circle was Paco. He untied Rocco's hands. No need for words, for shouting or ranting. Unable to look him in the eye, overpowered by his sorrowing gaze, the crowd shuffled silently away.

Bulldozer drew his knife.

'Who asked you to interfere? We were earning good money till you butted in!'

'Ah! Just what we need to cut this bread with!'

From the pockets of his cassock Paco produced a loaf and a bottle of wine.

'And when you've divided up the bread, see if you can get this cork out with the point of that thing.'

The bread was fresh, soft on the inside and crispy on the outside. Bulldozer sliced it in equal portions, then opened the bottle. He handed it to Rocco.

'You first.'

Rocco filled his cheeks to bulging with red wine. Thin jets spurted from the punctures in his flesh. The others cheered and clapped.

'Bravo, Rocco!'

Paco couldn't identify the undercurrent of noise coming from the discarded freezer, he only knew it was the sound of fear and distress. He lifted the lid. Hundreds of rats swept in dark tidal waves from one end of their prison to the other, piling up in pyramids against the walls, desperate to escape, fighting viciously to be at the top of the writhing heap. One, at least, made it over the top by scrambling on the backs of the others. Nelsón killed it with a blow from a stick. He turned the body over and spoke to it reproachfully,

'You see. It's no better on the outside after all.'

Another tried to escape over the rim and was clubbed to death. Nelsón tossed the body to the black-brown multitude.

'That's what I like about rats—you don't have to feed them, they eat each other.'

'Fathers eat their babies,' Angelina said.

'Elder brothers eat their younger sisters,' Angel added, nudging her playfully.

'And the big get bigger!' Nelsón crowed, holding a large one aloft by the tail.

Paco girded up his cassock and squatted on the ground. Bulldozer ostentaciously lit up a sucito of bazuko, exhaling loudly, fixing Paco with a defiant stare as he circulated it. Paco talked to them about football, about the price of glass and paper and about their lives, but never pressing the point when their answers were guarded or evasive. He offered them a cigarette each and had some paracetamol on him to quieten the pain of Rocco's injuries.

While Paco talked, his eyes followed Angel's hands as he made toys from odds and ends picked from the collecting bags. He had already made a kite and a simple motor car with two empty cans for front and back wheels, connected by a body of wire.

'Are they for sale?' Paco asked. Angel nodded.

'Thirty pesos each.'

Paco bought the tin-can car, saying with a wry smile that it reminded him of his own clapped out vehicle. As he stood up to go he saw that the slogan had reappeared on the brick wall, this time in even bigger letters.

'Ernesto Lives!'

There was a spring in Paco's step. Here was this little boy, amidst all this horror, creating something out of what had been rejected and discarded. 'Thank you, Lord. I had lost the way. Thank you for guiding me back to the path.' He turned. Angel was standing on a small mound of garbage, the kite on his back protruding on either side of his shoulders. Angelina joined him. With his sister's help, he lifted the kite off his back, fiddled with it for a moment, then set it flying, making it swoop and climb and twist, its multi-coloured tail-plumes fluttering in the air, soaring and dipping and soaring again.